LOVE FOR JUSTICE

Jonathan Stark

D1407654

1789 Legacy, LLC

This book is a work of fiction. Names, characters, places, and incidents are the product of the author's imagination or are used fictitiously. Any resemblance to actual events, locales, or persons, living or dead, is coincidental.

1789 Legacy, LLC
10168 Castlewood Lane
Oakton, VA 22124
www.1789Legacy.com

Printed in the United States of America
First edition: October 2016

1

Lonnie Perez lay comfortably on top of the bed in a rare moment of post-coital bliss. A fan in the window blew hot summer air across his naked body. He could hear Charlene down the hall in the bathroom. She'd be back soon and, for better or worse, this moment of peace would be over.

But now he savored it. Charlene wasn't bad for a second generation street man like himself. Her apartment was clean, even though the building wasn't, and she had a job, even though it didn't pay that great.

The toilet flushed about the same time somebody started pounding on the door. He listened. Years of experience screamed at him to grab his pants and run but that'd be the end of him and Charlene.

"Police, open up," said the voice in the hall. It was a deep voice, sounded like it belonged to a big man. With a gun.

"Will you get that, Lonnie?" asked Charlene. "I'm in the middle of something."

The pounding came again. It wasn't their door. It was across the hall.

"Hush up, Woman," said Lonnie. She flushed again.

This time the pounding was on their door. Lonnie jumped from the bed and had his pants on before he reached the window. More pounding, more calls to open the door. Now there was a woman's voice joining the man's. Lonnie hesitated for just a second, wondered what sort of woman owned that voice, a rich alto with a hint of something, maybe Latin? Shook his head. Didn't matter, she was a cop.

He pulled at the fan but it wouldn't budge. Another flush. "Lonnie, get the door!" said Charlene.

Lonnie kicked the fan out of the window. It clanged on something on the way down and then he heard somebody cry out in pained surprise. He looked out and saw a cop rubbing his head, kneeling beside a broken a fan.

"Sorry, Officer," said Lonnie. He dropped down beside the man. "Didn't know you were down here."

The policeman didn't move which, thought Lonnie as he appraised him, was good. The brother was fit and looked about six four.

Lonnie took stock of the scene and then darted down the alley. He slowed to a walk, and then a stylish loiter. The broken roadway was hot and sharp and his shoes were still upstairs in the apartment.

He figured Charlene would give them back if he asked her nicely, once the cops left. Or maybe she'd be mad and toss 'em after the fan. Either way, he'd have to wait.

Lonnie heard shouting and saw Charlene's neighbor's boy come running around the corner.

"S'up, Trey?" he asked. Trey grunted hello without slowing down. He was a skinny kid who could really move. Lonnie noted his running shoes with a bit of envy.

Three seconds later, the cop he'd hit with the fan flew around the corner after Trey. "Afternoon, Officer," said Lonnie, all casual. His eyebrows went up when he saw the back of the cop's vest. U.S. Marshal. That was Chuck Womack and he could move too, but his head was killing him from where a fan had struck it.

Chuck crossed the street after Trey, yelling for him to stop. Lonnie thought that was pretty funny.

When the second marshal came around the corner Lonnie pointed, "They went that way." Mitch nodded and huffed after. He was older and Lonnie didn't think he'd last long at that pace.

The third marshal around the corner was a few more seconds behind. It was the lady and Lonnie tipped his head before pointing down the street. Venus didn't even acknowledge him. She was moving faster than Mitch and looked like she could run down a train.

"Any more?" asked Lonnie, watching her backside fly down the alley. He saw Trey cut back across Dogwood, the marshals trailing behind, like a string of hound dogs after a rabbit. Lonnie got up and headed back to get his shoes but then thought better of it. Oh, that Charlene.

Dogwood Lane did not have any Dogwoods growing on it. Most of the houses were boarded up and the cars on the street didn't run anymore. But Trey was running.

Trey cut between two of the buildings and crashed through a ratty wooden fence. A pit bull dove at him but he dodged aside, tearing through the yard. Chuck was on his heels and tripped going through the fence, landed face to face with the dog.

It lunged for him but was snapped back by its chain. Mitch reached the fence and pulled Chuck up. They sprinted after the fugitive.

Trey leaped onto an old stove that had been conveniently pushed against a chain link fence, and vaulted to the alley beyond. The marshals followed. Venus caught up.

Between gasps, Mitch shouted at his Bluetooth. "Through to the alley, heading toward Birch."

"Be there in a second," said Pete. He wasn't out of breath, or even tired. The advantage of driving instead of running.

Chuck closed on Trey and dove for him at the intersection with Birch. He missed and Trey went south. A black Trailblazer blew onto the street, emergency lights flashing. Pete was at the wheel and hit the siren.

Trey skidded to a stop, no way out to either side. He ran back, crashing through Mitch and Venus. She got one of his arms but he twisted free.

"Heading north on Birch," said Mitch. He and Venus continued after Trey.

"I can see you," said Pete.

The Trailblazer skidded to a stop beside Chuck. The door flew open and Pete said, "Get in already." Chuck glared at the fat man driving but did as he was told.

Pete hit the siren again when they slid out onto Hemlock. It was a stylish move that sent an old woman driving a Caddy into cardiac arrest. They dove down the next cross street.

"Where are you?" asked Pete into his phone. "Do you see them?" he asked Chuck.

Chuck shook his head. They stopped at the cross street. "There," said Chuck, pointing. Pete gunned it and the truck leaped ahead. Chuck waved to Venus as they drove by. She ignored him, but Mitch raised a finger.

Trey hadn't opened up much of a lead but the foot pursuit hadn't closed on him either. Chuck bailed out when they were on him and the kid cut into another side yard.

"Are you kidding me?" asked Chuck resuming the chase. They climbed over another fence and crashed through trash cans. Trey forced his way through some broken slats in the back yard and took the alley through to Westbrook Ave.

Westbrook actually had traffic. Lots of it. Weird thing about the hood. As suddenly as you're in it, you're out of it.

Trey dodged across the street, cars skidding and horns honking. He jumped back a couple of times and the marshals closed.

A BMW 328i convertible was wedged between a U-Haul truck and an electrician's van. It was crowded with sorority sisters shopping for party smokes and blocked his path. He jumped into the car and hopped across them before continuing to Washington Boulevard along the park.

Pete beat him to it and pulled across the roadway. He aimed his Taser and took the shot. Trey jinked and the prongs missed. Pete tried an old Jedi mind trick to keep Trey still while reloading but it didn't work, the force was too strong with him. Trey dodged into the park and vaulted the low brick wall to the trees beyond.

Chuck and Venus followed him over, Mitch got into the truck. "Take the access road," he said.

"I know how to do this, Boss," said Pete. He looked left and right. "Which way is the access road?"

Mitch pointed and the truck sped down the street, sliding onto the access road and careening from pothole to pothole.

The trees opened into a pleasant rolling field filled with people enjoying the summer afternoon. Trey crashed across a picnic blanket scattering chips and soda cups. Chuck leaped it and the family stared wild eyed. Venus went around.

The three of them closed quickly on the basketball courts. Several games were in full swing inside tall chain link cages. Trey reached the fence and started to his right but Chuck was already there. He went left but saw the Trailblazer and hesitated.

Venus smashed into him, crushing him against the fence. He went down with her on top of him.

"Give me your hands!" she said. He gave her one, balled in a fist and moving at the speed of light. She dodged enough that he missed her nose but she still took the brunt of the shot.

"Oh, it's on." She threw her own punch, then another and before Trey knew what was up, a fusillade of fists, elbows, and knees told him about places in his body he didn't even know existed.

Trey stopped fighting when Chuck joined in. They cuffed him and dragged him to his feet as Mitch ran up. Mitch looked at Venus. "You alright?"

Venus spun Trey around and shoved him against the fence. "Didn't your momma ever tell you not to hit a girl?" she asked, deftly searching him for weapons and needles.

"Damn, you ain't no girl," said Trey. "You a marshal."

Venus dragged him to Pete's truck and shoved him inside. "You guys coming?" she asked.

Pete walked to the truck, looking over his shoulder at Chuck who was engaged in deep conversation with a young woman. "Yo, Chuckles. You ripped your shirt again."

Chuck pulled his shirt off to look. His upper body was Adonis chiseled in ebony. He glistened and, as if by magic, three more women appeared in the group.

Mitch climbed into the truck beside Trey, said to Venus, "How does he do that?"

"Because he's got it," said Venus. "Now are we going or what?"

Pete climbed in. Chuck kept talking. Pete hit the horn. Chuck waved him off. Pete hit the siren. Chuck looked at him, mouthed, "Just a minute." Then he took out his notepad and wrote down some numbers.

2

Katherine muted the GPS attached to the window of her rental truck. She couldn't take another soothing "Please make a safe and legal U-turn." Or a "gently merge left" for that matter. She had started her trip excited to have the company of Rodrick –– the name she'd given the GPS -- but now the robot who spoke the Queen's English like a well-mannered butler was getting on her nerves. And he reminded her a bit of the computer that killed all the astronauts in that Kubrick movie.

It was well after dinner time when she finally pulled to a stop in front of 14 Daisy Way. The house actually looked pretty nice but she had to pee so badly that a gas station restroom would have seemed like the Taj Mahal.

She bolted for the door, fumbled for a minute with the realtor's lock box, bouncing with her legs crossed, before finally giving up and running around back. She squatted between a ficus and the garage and smiled as her world was transformed.

It was a nice backyard and she didn't mind that her shoes had gotten a little damp. It only took her a minute to get the lockbox open this time around and she wandered into her new home. It wasn't big as houses go, but she was alone and it was easily four times the size of her Manhattan apartment.

She turned on all of the lights, made sure the fridge was working, then ordered take-out from the place her iPhone said was closest.

She carried a few boxes from the truck up the concrete path, across the front porch, and through the heavy front door. The boxes weren't labeled. She set them down in the room on the left.

It had a hardwood floor and a chandelier made of small globes done up in a faux iron style that clashed with the flower wall paper, but whatever. The boxes were heavy and she needed to find her clothes. So far all she'd found were dishes, books, and towels.

Back inside the truck she came face to face with a harsh reality. All of her friends were still in New York City. She'd known that all along and, except for Susan, she didn't really care. Except right now she needed to move her dresser and there wasn't anybody to help.

Katherine pulled out the drawers and stacked them neatly on her new front lawn, carful to put the jeans over the underwear. She tried to move the beast again but still no dice. She climbed over it and nearly got stuck when her foot went through a box filled with something that crunched if you put too much weight on it.

"On three," she said to the dresser.

She pushed hard. Heard creaks and cracks from the furniture at her back, was even able to make the top of the dresser wobble, but the base stayed firmly attached to the floor of the truck.

She cursed and felt better but claustrophobia was setting in so she climbed back over and sat on her couch, sweating and frustrated.

The food came in an old Nissan Sentra. "I'll give you ten bucks to help me get this dresser off the truck and into my house," she said.

The delivery man looked at her funny. "You ordered shrimp fried rice." She pointed to the dresser, then the front door, then waved a ten in the air. The man shook his head no, "Fried rice only." He ran back to the car.

Katherine sat back down on her couch inside the truck and ate her rice. There was a light on at 12 Daisy Lane so when she had eaten her fill, she walked over and rang the bell.

When the door opened, it revealed a handsome man in his late 70s sporting a full beard and wearing spectacles. "May I help you?"

She extended her hand. "Katherine Silver. I'm your new neighbor." His grip was light and his fingers were very smooth. "Do you know anybody around here who might be able to help me move some things out of the truck?"

He didn't and the way he said it made her think that perhaps this wasn't the sort of place neighbors paid much attention to each other.

The furniture was wedged in pretty tight. She struggled to pull out boxes and eventually was even able to free her mattress. It got dirty and ripped when she dragged it along the walkway, but at least it was in the house. She dropped that in the room on the right, a carpeted expanse with purple walls, recessed lights, and an electric fireplace.

Her phone rang. It was Susan. "How's it going?"

"I need a man," said Katherine.

"Already?" asked Susan.

"I can't get my dresser off the truck." Susan laughed at her. "I'm serious. My neighbor is about a hundred."

"You should have thought of that before you turned down Mark's offer to help you move."

"The whole reason I'm here is so Mark isn't," said Katherine.

"You okay?"

"Yes. Just thinking I didn't think this all the way through," said Katherine.

"You made the right choice."

"Except I don't have a man."

"You know how to get one of those," said Susan.

3

When Lonnie got to Big Maggie's place she was out on the porch swing sipping sweet tea. "Where you been?" she asked.

Lonnie thought about that and decided she was being polite so he gave the polite answer. "Catching up with some folks. Trying to stay out of trouble."

"Mmm hmmm," said Big Maggie. She had a special way of saying that. The sound sort of started deep down inside of her massive body and bounced around her gullet, up her neck where it shook her chins, and then purred out of her mouth through yellowed teeth.

"Got room for me tonight?" he asked.

She patted the swing next to her. "I always have room for you, Darlin'. You one of the good ones."

He gave her a quick kiss on the cheek and sat beside her. The swing creaked as she kicked her slippered feet against the floor.

"Where's your shirt?" she asked. "And your shoes?"

Good questions, he thought. "Do you really want to know?"

"Probably not. I've got some that will fit you in the back closet."

"Thank you." He was always on his best behavior with her. She didn't insist on it openly, but the rude brothers found their welcome worn thin pretty quick. "I'll get you some replacements."

"Mmm hmmm." She rocked in silence, watched the street and the night.

He watched with her.

"I gotta meet my P.O. tomorrow. Can I tell her I'm staying here?" he asked.

Big Maggie turned to face him. "You still on probation?"

He held his hands out. "A man like me is gonna be on probation his whole life."

"You got a good one this time?"

"She's not bad," said Lonnie. Actually, she was pretty good to him. Except for the drug testing. "Can you give me a ride?"

"That's what the bus is for."

He made a face. "You know the bus is only good for catching diseases and getting framed up. I ride the bus, I'll get violated for sure."

"You don't have the fare."

"Sure I got the fare," said Lonnie. He tried real hard to sound convincing.

"Then why's it you show up here barefoot and walking instead of riding the bus?"

Big Maggie was smart like that. Part of why he liked her. "You know I can't ask you for money."

"But I can give you some." She spoke like a cross between a big sister, an aunt, and a grandmother.

"I'll pay you back," he said.

"I know. You always do."

They rocked and she drank her tea. Lonnie thought about the marshals chasing Trey.

4

The marshals weren't thinking about Lonnie. They were drinking beer at Gillian's on Broadway because that's what they did on Tuesday nights.

The pub was a nice place, dark with dark wood tables, dark wood paneling, and a big, heavy, dark wood bar running along the wall with matching dark wood stools. The stools, chairs, and benches all had dark leather covers. The walls were covered with comfortable junk — hubcaps to parachute pants -- and a jukebox played "Night Ranger" at a volume that still allowed conversation.

The door opened and two uptight middle aged men in suits walked in.

"Look out everybody, the FBI's here," said Pete.

"Leave them alone," said Venus. "It isn't nice to make fun of things people can't help."

Kurt Cunningham was the agent in the blue shirt with the red power tie. The other guy was Robert Something-or-other. Kurt frowned at the marshals on his way to the bar.

Chuck turned around to watch them. "Man, they look unhappy."

Gillian passed a couple of bottles of Bud Light to the agents.

"You know that stuff has alcohol in it," said Pete. "Can you drink it while you're on duty?"

"We're not on duty, Genius," said Robert Something-or-other.

"He knows that," said Kurt. He picked up his beer and went to the pool table in back.

"No sense of humor," said Pete.

"Don't start with them tonight," said Mitch.

"Why not?" asked Pete.

"They can't help it if they didn't get to go outside today for recess," said Mitch. Venus shook her head.

"You know, you're right," said Pete. He stood up. "I'm going to go buy them a drink."

Mitch watched him go so he didn't see the door open but he did hear Chuck's intake of breath so he turned, hand moving toward his gun.

Katherine Silver stood in the doorway, assessing the place in a pair of faded jeans and a stained Columbia sweatshirt. Her hair was pulled back and some of it had escaped. She picked an empty spot at the bar and glided over to it, one eye and both hands on her iPhone the whole time.

"You know her?" Chuck asked Mitch.

"No," he said. "Should I?"

Chuck grinned. "You tell me, Cowboy. She looks like your type."

"You might want to go over and meet her before Pete gets back," said Venus. "If he arranges the introduction he'll charge you for a trick."

Mitch watched her. "It's a school night. I'm not really in the mood."

Pete sat down. "In the mood for what?"

Mitch answered quickly, "Nothing," and then added the diversion, "Did the FBI like their big boy drinks?"

But Chuck was faster, said, "Hottie that just walked in," with a gesture toward Katherine that was anything but discreet.

Pete followed the gesture and became thoughtful. "She looks familiar."

"Don't worry about it," said Mitch. They watched Kurt leave his partner at the pool table and saunter over to the bar. He took the stool next to her.

"He's putting the moves on your girl," said Chuck.

"She's not my girl," said Mitch.

"It's Kurt," said Pete. "Doesn't that automatically make her your girl?"

"That was one time," said Mitch. "Why can't anyone let that go?"

Venus laughed. "Probably because they were engaged before you came along."

"Want me to find out how serious this thing is between them?" asked Pete.

"I'm good, Big Daddy," said Mitch. He took a swig from his bottle. He tried to play it off. But he kept watching Katherine and she kept smiling at Kurt.

Chuck turned toward the couple. "Man, they sure are having a good time over there." Venus and Pete laughed.

"Fine. Kurt's married," said Mitch.

"He is?" asked Chuck.

"Oh, I just hate that. A nice girl is at the bar and you want to talk to her but you can't because some married dude is blocking you," said Pete.

"Chuck wasn't with us yet the last time you clowns pulled that one," said Venus.

Mitch and Pete got up. Pete put his hand on Chuck's shoulder, leaned down near his ear, and said, "Watch and learn, Chuckwagon. This is how we do things downtown."

Chuck nodded, very seriously. Then he and Venus burst out laughing. Pete shushed them and they tried desperately to hold it in.

Pete and Mitch walked over to the bar. Pete slid up next to Kurt while Mitch took a spot two stools over from Katherine.

Pete interrupted Kurt. "Hey, sorry about earlier. Can I buy you another drink?" Mitch got out his cell phone.

"I'm good," said Kurt.

"It's just that I feel bad, you know?" asked Pete. "We had such a great arrest today and I was sort of rubbing your face in it."

Kurt waved him off. "Don't worry about it, Kiddo. I'm kind of busy, why don't you take off?"

"Is this your sister?" asked Pete. He held out his hand to Katherine. "Hi, I'm Pete."

She was confused, but took his hand and they shook. "I'm Katherine." Behind her Mitch placed a call.

"You don't have to talk to him," said Kurt. Pete looked hurt.

"Why wouldn't I want to?" asked Katherine. Pete nodded, good question.

"Do you want all of the reasons or just the top five?" asked Kurt.

The bar phone rang and Gillian answered it while Pete said, "Gee, that really hurts." He patted his chest. "Right here."

Katherine laughed. "Why did you think I was his sister?"

Pete leaned in against the bar. "Clues." He paused to look at Kurt. "You know what those are, right? They're how investigators solve crimes?" Kurt scowled. Pete continued. "He rushed over here the second you walked in so it was like he either knew you or was really, really desperate. But, since he's married, I figured he wasn't looking for any action."

Katherine leaned back and looked hard at Kurt. "You're married?"

"I'm not married," said Kurt. "Don't listen to that man. He lies for a living."

Gillian walked over with the phone. "Kurt? I've got a call for you."

"Who is it?"

"It's your wife. Says you must have your cell off, she's been trying to get you for half an hour," said Gillian.

"But I'm not married," said Kurt. Gillian shrugged, handed him the phone, and walked away. Katherine watched, curious, while behind her, two stools away, Mitch spoke into his phone with a falsetto voice.

Kurt tentatively put the phone to his ear. "Hello?"

"It's your wife, Dear." said falsetto Mitch. He turned so that he faced Katherine and could see Kurt. "When are you coming home? Momma misses you."

Katherine turned to the sound of the falsetto, spotted Mitch, and her lips twitched. Mitch flashed her the smile, a million candle power of charm.

"This isn't funny," said Kurt. "Seriously. I'm hanging up now." But he didn't move the phone.

"Oh good, then you'll be home in time to watch the Designing Women marathon on Lifetime with me," said falsetto Mitch.

Katherine's twitch of the lips became a careful smile. Mitch hung up the phone and moved one stool closer to her.

"Really. This isn't funny. I don't think it's funny," said Kurt, not realizing the connection was already cut.

Katherine laughed and moved over a stool to sit by Mitch. Kurt realized what was happening and slipped off the stool but Pete put a restraining arm on his shoulder.

"Hey, Brother," said Pete. "That right there is another clue." Kurt glared at him, then at Mitch and Katherine. "Tell you what," continued Pete, "Let's you and me play a game of 9 ball."

Kurt shook off his hand and stomped back to Robert Something-or-other. Pete saluted Mitch and headed back to the marshals' table.

"How long have you been doing that routine?" asked Katherine.

"It's been in my family for generations," said Mitch. "My pappy learned it from his pappy who learned it from my great-grand pappy. But Pete and I have only been together for about ten years."

"You two an item?" she asked.

Mitch smiled. "We're not that kind of partners."

"Cops." The way she said it sort of made you think of taxes.

"Yes ma'am," said Mitch. "But not like that old oak."

"What do you have against the FBI?" she asked.

"Nothing," said Mitch. "When I get tired of closing cases and working for a living I plan to transfer."

"That's cocky," said Katherine.

Mitch saw she wasn't going for the line. "Maybe. It isn't really fair either. They work, I guess. But staring at spreadsheets at a desk all day isn't police work to me. I prefer the street."

"The grit and grime?" she asked.

"That and less paperwork. I don't have to worry about preserving evidence or proving intent. I get a piece of paper with somebody's name on it and bring that body back to the judge who asked for him."

"You don't have to worry about guilt or innocence," she said.

"Nope, everybody I chase is already wanted," said Mitch. "Somebody found them guilty and they ran from it. I bring them back. It's about Justice." He caught himself getting passionate, not where he'd planned on heading.

"A marshal."

"You say that like you need another drink," said Mitch, trying to get away from philosophy.

"Wow. That was smooth," said Katherine. "Are you going to ask me if it hurt next?"

Mitch mouthed it back to her, a puzzled expression on his face. "You know, when I fell?" she prompted. Comprehension dawned like a new morning.

"Naw," he said, waving her off. "How could falling out of heaven hurt if you never left? Clearly I'm there now."

She smiled at him. "That was okay. You can buy me a drink." She looked over at Kurt. "But only because I don't ever want that man over there to try anything with me again."

Mitch signaled to Gillian then followed her gaze to Kurt. "If we started making out that would pretty much take care of things."

"You move fast," she said.

"Life is short."

"Not that short," she laughed.

Mitch looked away, suddenly serious and the fun gone. "Sometimes it is."

Gillian dropped off the drinks. Katherine took hers and looked across the rim at Mitch. She was intrigued despite herself. He was far more complicated than the shtick suggested.

"Thank you for the drink," said Katherine.

Mitch turned back to her. He raised his glass. "To Justice. Thank God she's blind." Katherine smiled and raised her own glass.

"When you came over here, was it to make a play or just to chase away Kurt?"

"That's direct," said Mitch, his grin back in place.

She stared at him, clearly a serious question. He smiled, the normal everyday variety.

"It was about saving you," said Mitch. "A smile like yours is wasted on an ass like him."

Across the bar the marshals rose and pushed in their chairs. Venus waved. "See you tomorrow, Boss." He waved back. Checked his watch. Stood.

He was serious again. "It was nice to meet you -" and suddenly realized he didn't know her name.

"Katherine," she said, extending her hand. He took it.

"I'm Mitch. Maybe I'll see you around." He walked away and she watched him go.

"Maybe," she said to his back, her lips twitching again.

Gillian slid down the bar. "You okay?"

"I think so," said Katherine.

"New to my place or to the city?"

"The whole she-bang," said Katherine. "I'm just down from New York."

"Welcome. To the whole shebang." Gillian smiled.

"What's the story with the marshal?"

"Mitch? How much time you got?"

"That bad?"

Gillian thought for a moment. "He can be a real charmer but at heart he's good people." She wiped absently at the bar with her cloth. "A true believer."

"He seems to be a bit more than I expected from the phone bit," said Katherine.

Gillian snorted. "You be careful, Hun." She took Mitch's glass off the bar. "Kurt's not all bad. Mitch can be a dear, but those two have history. They're both larger than life and you don't want to be in the middle of that."

Katherine nodded. "I just got out of something larger than life. That's the last place I want to end up again."

"Good," said Gillian. "Then you're fine. It'll be a month before Kurt even thinks about talking to you again and if Mitch was going to make a play he'd have left with you."

Katherine was a tad offended. "What do you mean?"

"You saw his smile."

Katherine flushed and stared at her drink.

"He's irresistible and knows it, but there are only two types of women I've ever seen him with. Friends he hangs with that are always around, and the ones he meets here and leaves with. Never to be seen again."

"So he's a serial killer," said Katherine. Gillian just shrugged.

5

Trey stood in line for the phone. He wore an orange jumpsuit stenciled with "County Jail" on the back and the bored expression everyone adopted on the inside.

When it was his turn, he swiped his commissary card and dialed the only number he knew by heart. A collection of transfer stations and cell towers connected Jet to the other end of the dirty handset.

"Trey, that better be you," said Jet.

"It's me. Got picked up by marshals this afternoon. Court tomorrow."

"And that's my problem why, exactly?"

Trey didn't bat an eye. Jet liked to strut. "You can get me out or you can leave me in."

There was silence so Trey continued, "You're the boss. I do whatever you want."

"That's right. I'm the boss and you do what I want," said Jet. "I did not want you to get arrested."

"No, sir."

Another pause, this time Trey waited.

"Marshals. So fed court?" asked Jet.

"Magistrate. Probably in the afternoon."

"I know when it is, Convict," said Jet. Then he hung up.

Trey kept talking and nodding. He wasn't looking forward to the next part of his stay at County and the longer he was on the phone the longer he could put it off.

6

Katherine woke up a little bit after early and spent more time than she had planned trying to make coffee. By the time she was out the door it was already closing in on late.

She stopped short on her porch. This wasn't New York. There were no buses. There were no cabs. There were no people. She looked at the U-Haul truck still parked on the curb. She looked at her empty driveway. She looked at her watch.

After a last hopeful glance at the street for an alternative, Katherine went back into the house and returned a moment later with the keys to the U-Haul. It started on the second try.

7

Mitch parked his Harley behind the courthouse. It was an old building and looked a tad presumptuous. It was probably quite formidable and intimidating when it was built, but by today's standards it was small and overdone. Of course fashion comes and goes so it's possible that by the time you read this, the architectural style will be back in vogue.

The Warrants Squad had their office on the ground floor. You reached it by passing through a security checkpoint manned by retired cops wearing blue blazers and a smile for the ladies. Mitch walked through the metal detector, said good morning over the alarm, and headed left toward the rest rooms.

He stopped at a heavy door, locked and unmarked, fished out a key, and let himself in. Beyond that door was a small space and another door. This one had a card reader and a keypad. Mitch dutifully swiped his card and entered his code. He pulled open the door and entered a cramped space with four desks pushed together, alternating neat and cluttered. The walls were covered with wanted posters and a bigger than life depiction of Tommy Lee Jones daring anyone to mock Samuel Gerrard.

He booted up his computer and started in on the day's reports while he waited for the rest of the squad to filter in. Wednesdays were like that. No early morning hit, no pressure, no worries.

8

The OPS squad room was brightly lit with cream colored walls and dark blue carpet. Low cubicles ran in rows while the walls were lined with filing cabinets, whiteboards, and a huge digital schedule board. A pair of big screen TVs played 24 hours news on opposite sides of the room but no one seemed to pay them any mind.

A metal door with a corrections' grade lock was at one end of the room. Signs reading, "Authorized Personnel Only" and "No Weapons Beyond This Point" reminded casual visitors they were in a different world, surrounded by men and women who were armed and most definitely authorized.

Half the cubes were occupied by Deputy United States Marshals, the rank and file of the service referenced in shorthand as DUSMs. Some were in suits, the uniform of the day for producing prisoners in court, while others wore the ubiquitous 5-11 style pants of business-casual law enforcement and dark polo shirts emblazoned with the marshals' star.

Mitch slipped through the squad bay to the door of the supervisor's glass walled office. Steve Hart had made the switch to management by pronouncing, "I'm a man who now prefers meatball subs to foot chases."

"Hey, Steve-o," said Mitch. Steve looked up, his glasses crooked and a red mark on his cheek where he'd been leaning on his fist.

"Hey, Mitch," he said. "Good grab yesterday."

"Thanks," said Mitch. "Always good to get some fit time in."

"Now you can get some court time in too," said Steve. "Your boy is contesting. You'll have to testify at the identity hearing."

Mitch was incredulous. "He ran like 20 miles."

Steve shrugged. "Cindy just called it down."

"I thought Judge Johnson retired," said Mitch.

"He did," said Steve. "About six months ago. You really do live in a different world. Cindy's clerking for the new judge. Silver. You'll like her. She doesn't put up with any crap."

"Right." Mitch didn't buy that for a second. "Who's the AUSA?"

"Gaff," said Steve.

Mitch liked Assistant United States Attorney Terry Gaff. He was a regular guy who could talk about baseball and hunting as easily as case law and didn't have a fetish for his own voice. "Who's the public defender?"

Steve leaned back in his chair, fingers interlaced behind his head. "There isn't one. He's got private counsel."

Mitch nodded, very seriously, very sarcastically. "Right."

"Really." Steve leaned forward, folded his hands on his desk. Savored the moment. "It's Restrepo."

"You're putting me on."

"Court's at 2 in 6F. My guys will bring him up," said Steve. "Have fun."

9

Katherine sat at her new desk in her new office and looked across a collection of unpacked boxes and through the window beyond. The sun beckoned. She imagined herself walking on the street outside, part of the crowd passing her U-Haul.

There was a knock and she turned to see Cindy standing in the doorway. "Are you ready, Judge?"

She wasn't. "I'm not used to being called Judge," said Katherine.

"Put the robe on," said Cindy. "That will help." She walked in and took the robe off its hangar behind the door.

Katherine slipped it on. "How's that?"

Cindy bit her lip. "It's backwards."

Katherine flushed and started to take it off before she caught the other woman's smile. She flushed a little more.

"Sorry, couldn't resist." Cindy smoothed out the shoulders. "Now you look the part."

10

Mitch and Pete sat on a bench in the gallery of the court room. An old man in a blue coat dozed in the back, his name badge identified him as a court security officer, and two attorneys ignored each other at the counsel tables.

Terry Gaff wore an off the rack gray suit, hair cut short but not shaved the way most men with a bald spot like his would handle it. He had a single yellow legal pad laid out in front of him beside a thin manila folder. It was just another day in the office.

Ramon Restrepo was the sort of man who filled all of the available space around him, figuratively in life and literally at the defense table. He spread out books and folders and notepads, none of which had anything to do with the case but served to make him look extraordinarily busy and important. He also hoped it was a bit intimidating, but that was hubris. Most people thought he was a bit of a joke, though to be fair, he was a good attorney. His suit was a bespoke navy pinstripe and, naturally, he wore a yellow bowtie.

Trey was escorted from the holding area in his county uniform and full set of prison jewelry by a pair of deputy marshals. The man was Chris Sullivan, farm boy solid with rumpled blond hair and an even more rumpled suit. He had big feet and big expectations, new enough on the job that an afternoon in court was exciting. The woman was Marci Warren, patient the way an old dog puts up with a new puppy.

They settled Trey into a seat next to Ramon and took up positions behind him. Trey fidgeted, jangled his chains and scraped his cuffs on the table, Marley trying to get Scrooge's attention.

Cindy stuck her head out of the judge's door in the back of the court room. She smiled when she saw Mitch and waved. He waved back.

"Counselors, are we ready?" she asked. They were.

A moment later she reappeared and announced, "All rise." They all rose, except Trey who sort of extended slowly and grimaced as if it were the most painful thing he had ever done in his entire life.

Katherine walked to her seat at the bench and sat down. Cindy said, "You may be seated."

Pete elbowed Mitch. Mitch stared at Katherine. "I told you she looked familiar," said Pete.

Mitch nodded, slowly. "This isn't good."

Cindy turned on the recorder and said, "Court is now in session, the Honorable Katherine Silver presiding. The matter is the United States of America versus Treyton Rawlings. Counselors, please state your appearance for the record."

"Good afternoon. Terry Gaff for the government, Your Honor."

"Ramon Restrepo for the defense, Your Honor." He smiled at her, showed too many teeth. "Good afternoon."

"I understand your client has requested an identity hearing," said Katherine.

"That's correct, Your Honor," said Restrepo.

"Are you ready to proceed, Mr. Gaff?" asked Katherine.

"The government is fully prepared to prove that the man before you is Treyton Rawlings and that he is the same Treyton Rawlings wanted for violent drug related crimes."

Ramon became indignant. "Violent drug related crimes? We are asking for an identity hearing, not a chance for the government to audition an opening argument!"

"We will proceed with the hearing," said Katherine. She stared down the lawyers. "Gentlemen, please behave. I may be new to this bench, but I am not new to the law and will not hesitate to use my authority. Don't be my first example."

Mitch smiled. Steve was right, she didn't take any crap and as he watched her, that odd sense of being off-balance returned from last night. For her part, Katherine didn't seem to even notice he was present.

Terry stood and handed a document from his manila folder to Cindy. "Your Honor, the government would like to submit Mr. Rawling's post arrest report into evidence."

Cindy put a sticker on the document and handed it to Ramon.

Terry said, "Exhibit 1 is-"

Cindy cut him off. "We're using letters today."

Terry started again. "Exhibit A was generated downstairs in the Marshal's office following Mr. Rawling's arrest. It reflects a positive match of this defendant's finger prints with the Treyton Rawlings wanted for violating his supervised release by engaging in-" he looked over at Ramon – "criminal drug activity. I move to enter it into evidence."

Ramon made a big show of looking over the document, showed it to Trey, and then said, "No objection."

"Exhibit A is entered into evidence," said Katherine. "Do you have anything further?"

"Yes, Your Honor," said Terry. "I'd like to call Deputy Marshal Mitchell Kannenberg to testify."

"Marshal, you may approach," said Katherine.

Pete punched Mitch in the arm as he stood and walked through the swinging doors that separated the gallery from the counsel tables. He kept his eyes on Katherine, couldn't help it, and walked into the corner of the prosecution table. He grunted and fought to stay on his feet.

"Please state your full name and title for the record," said Cindy.

Mitch did, struggling. It was a painful hit.

"Marshal, you may be seated if you like," said Katherine.

He shook his head. "I'm alright." Trey cackled until Ramon shushed him, but he took his time doing so and his own face was marred by a smile.

"Proceed," said Katherine.

Terry stood and said, "How did you come to determine that the man seated at the defense table was Treyton Rawlings and return him to custody?"

Mitch kept his eyes on Katherine and too many different thoughts poured through his mind to speak at first. Finally, he said, "We received a lead with his pictures and some other stuff and -"

"Objection," said Ramon.

Katherine waited for more from the rotund man but there wasn't any. "In my court room you will have to provide the basis of your objections. There may be a presumption of innocence for the defendant, but not of competence for counsel."

"Of course, Your Honor," said Ramon, almost patronizingly. "The photo has not been entered into evidence."

"Over-ruled," said Katherine. "It's an identity hearing and we're receiving testimony from the arresting officer." She looked over at Mitch, maybe for the first time. Her lip twitched. "Please relax, Marshal. And continue."

Mitch got his bearing and started again, confident. "Right. We developed information based on standard investigative techniques that the man wanted in the warrant was staying at his mother's place. We went to the address and the defendant was there. He matched the physical description of the wanted subject, including a photograph, so we approached and identified ourselves as police." He stared at Ramon but the lawyer ignored him.

"And then what happened?" asked Terry.

"He fled," said Mitch. "We told him to stop but he kept running."

"Did he have any identification when you caught him?" asked Terry.

"No."

"Did he provide a name to you at any time?" asked Terry.

"When I processed him I asked his name and he said, 'Will Smith.' I told him that he knew the drill and I needed a name for the forms. He said, 'You know my name.' but didn't provide anything further."

Terry made a face. "Is it common for criminals to make up names during processing?"

"Happens all the time," said Mitch. "We put them in and a list of aliases gets attached to the finger prints."

Terry asked, "Did the fingerprints match Trey Rawlings?"

Mitch nodded. "Yes."

Ramon spluttered at Mitch for a bit when the AUSA had finished but it was all show. There was no question that his client was the wanted man. He saved most of his energy and surprising bit of charm for the detention hearing which followed.

The government sought detention, argued that the defendant had already proven he was a flight risk and was a convicted drug dealer. Ramon pointed out that no drugs were recovered on his client who had simply been visiting his mother and didn't realize there was even a warrant until he was so forcefully taken into custody.

After several minutes of back and forth, Judge Katherine Silver gave in and, despite what she thought she'd do when it was her turn to be on the bench, she set release conditions. She set the bond high, but not high enough.

11

Jet sent the best dressed and least smelly member of his posse into the courthouse to post bond for Trey. He figured the feds could suspect him all they wanted, but if he never wrote a check himself they'd have a hard time saying he was the money man.

Jet was wrong, but the feds didn't really care about a small fry like him so it was sort of moot. He sat in the back of his Hummer and played Candy Crush on his phone. Stupid game. He hated it. Hated that he spent money on it. Hated that the chocolate just messed up his game and he'd lost. Again. It soured his mood.

He looked out the window and saw Trey walk out of the courthouse with another man. "Who's that cat?" asked Jet.

Wiggins rode shotgun most days. Today was not exceptional. He said, "That's Lonnie."

"I don't like him," said Jet.

"Aww, he's not so bad," said Wiggins. "Helps a man out of jam, you know?"

"So he's cool?" asked Jet.

"Is by me," said Wiggins. "Used to see him at Big Maggie's."

Jet pondered that while he put down his window. "Yo, Trey. Let's go."

Trey looked around until he saw the Hummer and waved. "See you round," he said to Lonnie.

"Be cool," said Lonnie. They shook in the funky way you learn when you're inside and need to know who your friends are.

Trey footed it over to the Hummer and climbed in the back. Jet offered him a can of mixed nuts and a water. Trey took them both. "Thanks, Jet."

"What were you and Lonnie talking about?" asked Jet.

Trey paused, mouth full of nuts, "You know Lonnie?"

Jet waited. Everybody knew he was the one who asked the questions. Trey gulped down the mouthful.

"He was in to see his P.O.," said Trey. "She says he needs to find a job or he's gonna be violated."

They all watched Lonnie. He stood on the corner of Pearl, right out in front of the courthouse. He greeted all the fancy suits that walked by and tipped his forehead to all the lady folk.

"What's he doing now?" asked Jet.

Trey shook his head. "Man, you don't know nothing. That brother is looking for a ride."

Wiggins turned around in his seat and gave Trey a harsh look.

"What?" asked Trey. "You know he don't. Not about the street."

"Even so," said Wiggins, "You should have a bit more respect."

Trey made a face but kept his mouth shut. Jet watched Lonnie.

"Then let's give the brother a lift," said Jet.

The Hummer moved up a block and stopped next to Lonnie. Trey got out, held the door, and motioned for Lonnie to climb in. The man was hesitant.

"Please," said Jet. "Let me give you a lift."

Wiggins nodded to Lonnie. "It's cool."

Lonnie climbed into the truck and squeezed next to Jet. Trey got in after.

"Give our guest those nuts," said Jet. Trey grabbed a handful and held out the can to Lonnie.

"No thank you," said Lonnie.

"A man offers you his nuts, you take them," said Trey.

"I don't want to be beholden," said Lonnie. He turned to face Jet. "Thank you for the ride."

"Where you headed?" asked Jet.

"I guess that depends on where we're going."

12

Mitch found his way to the operations squad room after court. His leg was killing him from where he had smashed against the table and he was still in shock from seeing Katherine and finding out that Trey was out on bond. A couple of DUSMs shot the breeze near the cellblock door but otherwise the place was empty. Steve was folded over his desk behind the glass.

Mitch lurked in Steve's doorway. "Steve-o."

"Hey ya, Mitch," said Steve. He didn't look up. "What's going on?"

"Just being social," said Mitch.

"Really, what do you need? Was court okay?"

"Yeah, it was fine," said Mitch. "I'm really just being social."

"You can sit down if you want, but I have to get this airlift manifest done," said Steve.

"Remember when your job was fun?"

Steve looked up. "I remember that I didn't have to get up at 3 am today."

"You used to have passion," said Mitch.

Steve snorted. "That reminds me, the new kid wanted to talk to you. Said he's got a lead or something."

"See? That's what I'm talking about. Leads. Not Con-Air prisoner lists."

"Whatever. They're in hooking up the return load. I'm done with him after that."

The cellblock door opened, released Chris and Marci back into the relative freedom of a job working for The Man. Chris spotted Mitch and came over.

"Hey, Sir," said Chris. "You have a minute?"

"Sure." Mitch followed the kid to his cubicle.

"I've been working on that Dmitry Anders case you gave me and I think I've got a good lead." He pulled out a blue case folder and flipped through the pages until he found the one he wanted.

"I'm listening," said Mitch.

"I did the usual computer checks and found an old girlfriend in Philly who said he was always working out and-"

Mitch cut in, "When did she say that?"

"When I called her." Chris wondered if Mitch was really all that. "Anyway, she said he was always at the gym picking up girls and bringing them back to the apartment while she was at work and that's why she kicked him out."

"Not much of a lead."

"Except that she said he had a membership with Total Body Workout so I checked out the one over on McGloin and turns out he's there almost every night at 7."

"How'd it turn out that way?" asked Mitch.

"I showed the picture to a girl who works over there."

"You don't think she'll tip him off?"

"No," said Chris. "She was stoked about helping out. I didn't show her the picture until I was sure she was being straight and, well, she pinky promised."

"Pinky promised?" asked Mitch. "They teach you that at the academy?"

"Pete said that was the way to do it." Chris looked quizzically at Mitch. "Is that alright?"

"If Pete said so," said Mitch. "You want to go over there tonight?"

"Yes, Sir."

"Who else do you have lined up?" asked Mitch.

"Just Marci." He looked at the two DUSMs in the corner. "Everybody else has little league practice."

One of the DUSMs looked over at them. "It's ballet, not little league."

The other one laughed. "These FNGs don't know the difference between a bat and a tutu."

Mitch laughed. "Okay. I'll get somebody from the squad. Just one thing."

"Yes sir?" asked Chris.

"Only call me sir in front of Pete." Mitch headed out, another day another dollar.

Chris said, "It's not too late if you guys want to come." They laughed at him.

He walked to Steve's office. "Do you mind-"

Steve cut him off with a wave. "Go." Chris bounced out leaving Steve with the manifest and the start of a migraine.

13

Jet's Hummer pulled up to the Speedy Rasheedy copy center on Afton near the Shaking Weasel club. Wiggins opened his door but Jet stopped him.

"You stay. Trey's got this." Jet looked at Trey. "Don't you, Trey." Trey made a face but got out of the truck and walked inside.

"You picking up business cards, Mr. Jet?" asked Lonnie.

"Please, just Jet," said Jet. "What we do here is collect cash from a business partner."

Lonnie nodded. "I do like clean money."

"And I like a man who knows what's what," said Jet. "I have a position for a man like that." A moment passed between the two of them.

Wiggins said, "He's coming back out." Jet looked up.

Sure enough, Trey was already coming back. "Your man wasn't in," he said, climbing back inside.

"And the money?" asked Jet.

"No man, no money."

"He didn't leave it for us?" asked Jet.

"No."

"Did you check in back?" asked Jet.

"I know how to do this," said Trey.

Wiggins said, "Awful fast to have checked in back."

"Shut up," said Trey.

Jet frowned. "I need that money."

"It's not there." Trey crossed his arms. A squad car slowed next to the double parked Hummer. The officer inside gave Jet's driver a hard look.

"Probably time to go," said Wiggins. They did. Jet was in a mood. He put the lid on the can of nuts. Lonnie tried to make himself smaller.

"See, thing is, that money's spoken for," said Jet. "And it's really easy to get. You just walk in and pick it up."

"Done it a thousand times," said Trey. "Except this time the man wasn't there and neither was the cash."

"You keep saying that. Stop saying that," said Jet.

"I'm just saying, is all," said Trey.

"Well don't," said Jet.

"Okay."

"It's not okay. You don't have my money."

"That's because..." Trey stopped, lost. "I never had your money and it wasn't where I was supposed to get it."

"I need my money. Where is it?"

"We could swing by Milton's," said Wiggins. "He's usually got some."

Jet smiled. "See how easy that is?" Trey didn't see but had enough sense to keep his mouth shut this time. They headed over to Milton's.

14

Mitch walked out of DeliMax with his dinner in a white paper bag. He crossed the street and saw Katherine walking out of the courthouse.

"Hello, Judge," he said.

She turned to see who it was. "How's your leg?"

Mitch wasn't expecting that. Or for her to keep walking after saying it. Did he let it go or fall in step? While he was thinking about that he started walking with her.

"Yeah, that was kind of embarrassing," he said.

"It certainly got my attention," she said.

"It got mine too." He smiled at her.

"Maybe you could work that into your routine at the bar?" She didn't slow, but she did look at him while she talked. "I trust there was no permanent damage?"

"No, Ma'am."

"Nothing that is going to require you to see a doctor?"

"No, Ma'am."

"Or miss work?"

"No, Ma'am."

"What about scarring or psychological damage?"

"No, Ma'am." He was lost. She was asking too many questions too quickly and was too gorgeous.

"And your repetitive speech," she paused, "Was that caused by your accident?"

"No ma- I mean, no."

She laughed. "Then you don't have any grounds for a law suit. Looks like you'll just have to suck it up."

She stopped beside a U-Haul truck. "Are we parked next to each other?" He stared at her while she fished for keys. Was that seriously her ride?

"My bike's over there," he said, pointing to the Harley.

She pointed to his bag. "How you going to carry that?"

"I'm working late tonight. We've got a hit, I mean arrest, later."

She reconsidered him. "That's a long day."

He shrugged. "What we do for the love of justice, right?"

She nodded. "Be safe out there, Marshal Kannenberg." She climbed into the U-Haul. "There could be tables hiding anywhere."

Mitch watched her drive away, still in a bit of a haze. She'd remembered his name.

She glanced back in the mirror and swore softly. She forgot to ask him to help unload the truck.

15

Big Maggie watched a white Hummer, tricked out with 24 inch chrome spinners, a rainbow of neon, and dark tint, boom-bah its way down the street. "Where you headed, Gangster?" she asked softly.

It stopped in front of her house. She frowned.

The back door opened, spilled out Lonnie and some fiercely terrible homespun rap. Lonnie waved to the brother and white man inside then gently shut the door. He walked up the path to Maggie. He was all smiles until he saw her face.

The Hummer drove away. "I don't like that boy," said Big Maggie.

"Jet?"

"That what the devil calling himself these days?" asked Big Maggie. "That there is trouble."

"You got to dance with trouble if you want to get ahead in this world."

Big Maggie snorted with her whole body. "That sounds like a scheme. You roll with that crew and you find yourself a new place to sleep."

Lonnie watched the Hummer turn at the end of the street, the spinners whirling, catching the light. Gave him a sort of a headache. But it also got him spinning, in his head. He'd been working an angle with the crazy white boy, but maybe a scheme was better.

"How about you trust me," said Lonnie. "And I'll make sure you don't have to worry about food for everybody."

Big Maggie pinched his cheek like he was some kind of 12 year old she ran into at church. "You don't fool me with your sweet talk. You start dealing and you're out."

"I know the rules."

16

Wiggins asked Jet if he thought they should drive around the block, give Milton a chance to get ready for the visit. Jet thought about that for a bit. Then Wiggins said he needed to decide quick because if they were going to go straight up they'd need to park just ahead.

"What do you think, Trey?" asked Jet.

"Stop asking me questions. You're in charge, make a freaking decision."

Jet gave him the eye. "You seem to have a respect problem."

Trey shook his head. "We going up to get the money or not?"

"Straight in. We'll surprise him," said Jet. He patted his suit coat where it covered a nickel plated 1911 style .45 automatic snug and secure in a Miami Classic.

Milton's place was rocking, for a crack house. The hip hop blasting through the broken windows shook the house and the neighboring structures. Nobody cared. It was an abandoned section of town, long ago given up by the city fathers with their Churchill cigars and Audis.

A junkie, lost in his own world and covered with puke, stumbled into the road in front of the Hummer.

Jet's driver hit the brakes. The can of nuts slid off the back seat and spilled. Jet jumped out of the truck, murderous rage in his eyes. Wiggins was on his heels and held him back.

"That guy doesn't even know where he is, Boss," said Wiggins. "We'll go inside and get your money, not waste time on this fool."

Jet nodded. "Yeah, inside for the money." He led the way, Wiggins and Trey flanking with flat black M4 carbines on slings.

The stoop crumbled under foot. The door didn't even swing. The smell was nearly overpowering. Jet hesitated.

"That's what street smells like," said Trey.

Jet turned on him. "I know what street smells like."

"We can take care of this," said Wiggins.

Jet pushed into the darkness. The place was falling apart, holes in all of the walls, the floor broken up, and bodies everywhere. Or piles of junk. It was hard to tell ruined recliners from crack-heads sharing a moment.

Jet stepped over all of them. Few people noticed them. One or two might have tried to get up and leave, but it was hard to tell. They were glassy eyed and far away and beneath his notice.

The three men climbed the stairs to the grand room, a full length space made by the intentional removal of the partition and load bearing walls.

"Fool's gonna bring down his own house," said Wiggins.

Jet picked his way through the trash covered floor. Milton watched him come, ensconced in an old leather wingback with a scrawny chick on his lap and two lackeys at his back. He was a dark black in his middle 20s, portly and shaved bald. He drank from a glass instead of a can.

The revelers upstairs were a bit cleaner, still stoned, but not as far gone. Most of the sycophants retreated to the shadows when they noticed the long arms. A few stayed to see what the white boy was after.

"Jet," said Milton. "What an unexpected surprise." He gestured to a folding table in the corner of the room. It was covered with cheap alcohol. "May I offer you refreshment?"

"Only if by refreshment you mean cash," said Jet. He was proud of the line but nobody laughed. Trey was getting on his nerves.

Milton frowned. "I'm not sure what you're talking about."

"I'm here for my money," said Jet.

"But you don't get your money here," said Milton. "And you don't get it today. Our arrangement is for Tuesday."

"I am here. And I get my money today."

Milton shooed the girl off his lap and stood. He was tall. Jet had to look up. That pissed him off. He wanted to tell the man to sit, but he'd just told him to get the money.

"Mr. Rask," said Milton, "Do you have any idea how rude it is to come into my establishment with your thugs and your guns and threaten me in front of my clients?" He took a step closer.

"You pay, we leave." Jet noticed 9mms in the waistbands of the kids behind Milton. They probably didn't know how to use them, but even a blind squirrel gets a nut once in a while.

Milton shook his head. "You leave now. Then I pay on the day we agreed. At the place we agreed." He crossed his arms. The two kids behind him drew their guns and aimed in the general direction of Wiggins and Trey.

Jet couldn't believe it. "Who do you think you are? Drawing down on my men?"

Milton spoke very softly. "Who do you think you are, waltzing in here all SWAT? You dishonor me, and why? Because you're a punk. A nobody just wanting to be somebody. You aren't street. You aren't hood. You're a poser. A rich boy pretending to be somebody else. You're nothing, you hear?"

Milton fell back onto the floor, a pair of holes in his forehead where the slugs from Jet's 1911 pistol entered his skull. The back of the head was a mess, but that was on the ground and hidden from sight. While Jet was most of what Milton had said, he was not all show.

"Nothing?" he asked the corpse. "I'm Jet Rask you disrespectful son of a bitch." He shifted his pistol back and forth between Milton's guards.

Trey looked at Wiggins. Wiggins shrugged, had his M4 raised to his shoulder aimed comfortably at the closest of Milton's thugs. Trey raised his rifle. The kids looked at them, Milton, finally Jet, and dropped their pistols.

"Now, who wants to get me my money?" asked Jet.

17

The Total Body Workout on McGloin was the ground floor of a renovated warehouse that had been converted from self-storage units a few years back. The upstairs was supposed to be condos for the up and coming, but somewhere along the way the developer changed plans and now it was vacant. The outside was awash in neon, promising a new body and new attitude starting at just $49 per month.

Mitch and Chris waited in a tinted out black Explorer parked a discreet distance from the entrance. They wore windbreakers over their vests and America's Star hung around their necks.

A few hundred yards away Pete and Marci waited in a silver Charger. Marci was resigned to a night of waiting but Pete was antsy and his stomach was giving him trouble.

The door opened and closed regularly for a stream of people in spandex and earbuds. Mitch didn't get it. Everybody was dressed like they wanted to be noticed but nobody seemed to be paying anyone else any attention. He was hunting. Noticed them all and discounted them as quickly.

Chris broke his concentration. "Can't believe I'm here. Doing this."

"Welcome to the big time, Kid," said Mitch. He kept scanning.

"Cool." Chris looked at Mitch. "But it isn't really the big time."

"What do you think the big time is?" asked Mitch.

"It's, you know, real cases. Big time."

"We're man-hunting," said Mitch. "What's more big-time than that?"

"Just saying, this case. It isn't really big time," said Chris. "Right?"

"First case can't be big time?" asked Mitch. "Listen, this is a good case. Most of our warrants are supervised release violations so you can't judge it by that. You've got to look at the person behind the charge, the underlying. You've got an animal here."

"Really?"

"Sure," said Mitch. "I don't believe in wasting time on junk for new guys. If you're a hunter, you're a hunter. Either you can do the work or not."

Chris grinned, like he'd just gotten invited to the prom. "So this is the big time."

Mitch pointed. "That guy in the blue t-shirt?"

Chris shook his head. "Not even close."

"Good," said Mitch. "See, Chuck? He would have bailed out on that guy. Taken him down. Dragged him to booking and then argued that the computer was wrong when it told him he had the wrong guy."

Chris laughed. "He's really that bad at picking people out?"

"He's a genius with the computer, but can't pick faces for anything."

"Where is the squad anyway?" asked Chris.

"Where are the OPS guys?" said Mitch.

"Nobody wanted to come, you saw that." Chris looked back out the window. "I don't get it. This is a good lead. Why don't they want the break from court?"

"A break from court is doing this during the day. You're asking them to skip out on family time," said Mitch. "Little League practice."

They laughed. Chris said, "But wouldn't you rather be out here catching a bad guy than sitting on your couch watching someone else do it on a rerun?"

"That's why I'm here."

"I guess I just don't get why nobody else wants to be here. We've got the best job in the world," said Chris with a bit of the True Believer sneaking out in his voice.

Mitch said, "Your boss? He's got five kids. How long is that family going to last if he's out the door at 4am and doesn't get back until after bath time?"

Mitch trailed off, staring at a weightlifter. The comms radio cracked to life. It was Pete, wanted to know what they thought of the guy in black.

Mitch snagged the blue case folder from Sullivan and flipped through it, finger sliding along height and weight. Noted the tattoo again and stared back at the cold eyes of the mugshot. "This guy's too small," he said into the radio. "Height is good, but Anders is heavier."

Pete said, "Marci wants to know if we're talking heavier muscle or heavier gut."

Chris watched the lifter walk away, anxious to go hands on. "You sure our guy is bigger than that?"

Mitch nodded, said into the radio, "Tell her the first. He's built more like me than you.

"Yeah, ha ha." said Pete. "I forgot how funny you are on stakeouts. Let's stop him. I think that's our guy."

"He's not our guy," said Mitch. "You need to think bigger."

"Come on, I'm serious. I think that was our guy."

Mitch said, "Wasn't our guy, Chuck."

Pete didn't appreciate that. "Whatever. It's been a long day and I don't want to sit out here all night."

"It'll be fun," said Mitch. "You can tell our young friend all about your first arrest."

"That's alright. Hey, do you see that guy?"

They did. Both Mitch and Chris watched a broad shouldered Dmitry Anders lumber toward the entrance of the gym, running shoes on his feet and a torn sweatshirt barely containing his massive torso.

Sullivan said, "That's him." He reached for the door.

Mitch stopped him. "Slow down, Cowboy. You see how big he is?"

"What's the play?" asked Pete.

Mitch said, "We wait. Let him wear himself out inside first."

Pete came back over the radio, said, "We should go now. We're tired of waiting." Mitch heard Marci in the background denying every word. Actually, she said something like, "I'm not fighting that guy."

"We're not going to the hospital tonight," said Mitch. "We're waiting."

"We've got a Taser, we can take him," said Pete.

Sullivan looked at Mitch, said "I don't have a Taser." Mitch grabbed for the case in his backseat. It wasn't there.

"You have one in your car?" asked Mitch. "Somebody didn't return mine. Pete."

Marci came back, "We don't have one." Then she yelled at Pete who had obviously climbed over the seat looking. "Those are my workout clothes, get out of there."

Sullivan bounced in his seat. "You sure we can't take him?"

"We can take him," said Mitch. "But it would hurt and I don't want to lose any more teeth." That settled the kid down. He liked his face, did well with his face. A scar might enhance his game, but missing teeth wouldn't.

Marci came back again. "Pete says you're getting soft."

Mitch said, "10-4," and put down the handset. "Give him half an hour then go in and make sure that's our guy. Try not to spook him." Sullivan nodded. "Hear me?" There was a lot of adrenaline in the way, but the kid heard.

18

Jet's Hummer wound its way through an upscale hood north of the city. The drives were all paved and the smallest house was over four-thousand square feet. The grounds were landscaped and had those iron looking lamp posts for some extra class.

They turned up a driveway marked by brick flowerbeds and the statue of a jockey. He was painted blue and yellow with white pants. Was probably somebody famous, Wiggins thought, but he didn't care for horses.

"We're here, Boss," he said. Jet crammed another handful of nuts into his mouth and brushed his hands off on his suit pants. The Hummer swung around the circular drive and stopped just in front of the door.

Wiggins, Trey, and Jet climbed out. Trey went around back and grabbed a rifle. "Did I tell you to get that?" asked Jet. Trey shook his head. They stared at each other for a minute. Trey was sick of the game. But he put the gun back.

Wiggins rang the bell and then stepped back so Jet was first. A girl of about 12 opened the door. She was mixed Indian and white, wore a Hollister sweatshirt over blue jeans. Cute kid. Jet pushed her out of the way.

A woman named Connie, in her late thirties and yoga pants, came into the hallway. She had long blond hair pulled back in a ponytail and stopped short when she saw Jet. "What are you doing in my house?"

"I'm here to see Raj."

"Get out." Wiggins admired how she stood up to Jet. Trey picked his nose. Wiped his finger on the pinstripe wall paper.

Jet stepped toward her. She stepped back. "Raj? Jet's here."

An Indian man in his middle sixties stuck his head out of the room at the end of the hall. He was still in his suit but the necktie was gone. "Mr. Rask."

"Where's my money?"

Connie looked at Raj. The little girl watched Trey digging in his nose for seconds. Raj looked in the general direction of Jet. "It's okay, Honey. Why don't you go upstairs?" He motioned for Jet to join him at the end of the hall.

Jet passed Connie and in a little voice said, "Why don't you go upstairs, Honey." She made a face at him and he glared at her. She withered a little. Wiggins and Trey followed him, Trey taking a moment to smear the booger on an antique side table that cost enough to cover his bail.

Raj led them into his den. It was nicely appointed, lots of leather and art, pictures, crystal and stone statues, and an empty fireplace. French doors opened out into the backyard.

Raj gestured to a couch and some chairs. "Bourbon?"

Jet looked at Wiggins. "The man offers me a drink. Did I tell him I wanted a drink?"

Wiggins said, "No."

"What did I tell you I wanted?" asked Jet.

"You want your money," said Wiggins.

Jet turned to Raj. "That's right. I want my money."

Raj fidgeted with his hands, noticed, and shoved them in his pockets. He didn't like Jet. The boy's father? Sure, they had a long history together, but this kid was a punk.

"First of all, it's your father's money. Secondly, you have no right to barge into my house like this and demand anything." Raj walked to where a crystal decanter sat on a tray. He willed himself to be calm. Carefully poured two fingers into a tumbler. "I offered you a drink to be polite."

"I'll take one," said Trey.

Everybody stared at him. Raj raised his eyebrows but poured another. He handed the tumbler to Trey. Jet watched Trey. Now that he had the glass he wasn't sure what to do with it. He set it down.

"No, please," said Jet. "Drink it."

Trey picked up the tumbler, threw back the dark brown liquid. Wiped his mouth. Jet turned away from him.

Raj asked, "Why are you here?"

Jet got all friendly, casual even. "See, we went to the shop, like usual. Went inside, like usual. Talked to Amir, like usual. Only thing, Raj, the money wasn't there."

Raj said, "As I explained to your father earlier, I don't have the money. My accounts were frozen."

"Why is that my problem?" asked Jet. "You are supposed to give me money. I stopped by the store to pick it up and it wasn't there."

"It's your problem," said Raj, "because I can't get to the money to give you."

Jet looked over at Wiggins. "Sounds more like it's his problem." Wiggins nodded. Trey had put on sort of a dumb, not quite with it, look.

Raj shook his head. "Fourteen years I've worked for your father. There's never been a problem. You know me. When I say there's a problem, there's a problem."

Jet thought for a minute. "Those accounts really frozen?"

"Yes."

"Feds are on to you?"

"All I know is what the bank told me, the funds are frozen." Raj sipped his bourbon.

"So they watching your house too?"

Raj didn't know. Hadn't thought that far ahead. Agents had come into the shop today to talk to him but he'd gone out the back. Probably wasn't a good idea to mention that.

Jet watched Raj working things out. "You trying to play me?"

Raj denied it. Jet said, "I don't like being played." Raj said he wasn't playing. Jet said, "I'm not playing either. You bring the heat on us and I'll bring all hell on you."

Raj believed him. "I will give you your money as soon as I can get to it. Like I said, I spoke with your father"-

Jet slapped him, hard. "My father isn't here. I'm tired of you talking about my father. You are supposed to give ME the money." Now Raj cowered. Jet slapped him again. It was loud and made his hand sting.

"Give me what you have here."

Raj said, "I don't keep any here." Jet looked around. The room smelled like money.

"I'm looking at money. You've got a stash. Hand it over."

Raj shook his head. Jet moved, fast, grabbed the decanter and smashed it on Raj's hand. It shattered against the desk through the man's hand.

Raj screamed. Pieces of glass flew everywhere. Some of it stuck out of the hand. The whisky burned as it flowed over the wound. Raj whimpered.

"Want to try that again?"

Raj didn't want to try it again and said as much. Jet walked around the room, pointing, speaking softly. "Is it here? How about here? Over there?"

Connie came in, saw Raj, and rushed over to him. Jet caught her halfway across the room and swung her at Wiggins. She was caught up in strong arms and found herself against a powerful man who smelled surprisingly good.

"Let her go," said Raj.

Jet laughed. "You don't like that?" He reached out and stroked her cheek. She tried to bite him and he slapped her playfully.

"Please," said Raj. Connie didn't speak. She grunted and strained against Wiggins but the man held her tight.

"What about this?" asked Jet. He ran his hand down the front of her t-shirt. Raj didn't like that. Neither did Connie and she spat at him. This time there was no play when he hit her, hard in the stomach. She doubled over.

"Alright." Raj went to a bookshelf near the fireplace and swung out a door. Behind it was a safe. It took him three tries to get it open. Trey collected the loot.

Jet wanted to know if there was anymore. Raj said no. Jet broke a jade Buda on his good hand but the answer didn't change, just the volume of his moaning.

Wiggins threw Connie over to where Raj lay crumpled on the floor. Then they left.

19

Dmitri Anders lingered at the reception desk on his way out. It was a waste of time, the girl behind the counter wasn't interested. He put his earbuds back in and walked out into the night. His bag felt heavy, he'd gone hard and it felt good.

He walked slowly, texting as he drank testosterone harvested from bulls out of a water bottle. He didn't see the tinted out Explorer or the two men who got out of it.

He did notice a man on the sidewalk in front of him but didn't pay any attention until he tried to go around and the man moved in front of him. Anders looked up.

He saw the badge. And the cuffs. And the scruffy old man behind the kid that was in his way. He looked back and saw a man and a woman, also with badges. Heavy night.

The kid was talking. He pulled his ear buds out and caught the end, something about putting out his hands. He did. Felt the cold cuff come down and then spun when the kid did something with his wrist that hurt more than he expected. The second cuff went on.

Mitch said, "That's great, Kid. Except how you going to get his bag?" Anders chuckled. His gym bag was still on his shoulder, strap caught in his arms.

"Oh yea," said Sullivan. He opened a cuff, yanked off the bag, and hooked Anders back up. Sullivan did a quick pat-down. The kid had a light touch. Missed the wallet. Anders told him. Kid went back in and fished it out. "Anything else?" Anders said no.

Mitch picked up the wallet and pulled out a driver's license. Dmitry Anders. "This yours?"

Anders nodded. "Did you know you were wanted?" asked Mitch. Anders nodded again.

Pete asked, "You high?"

Anders shook his head. Marci rounded up the iPhone and drink bottle. Dropped them in the gym bag. "You got anything sharp on you? Any contraband they won't take at county?" she asked.

"No. Just what you see."

Sullivan squatted down, started going through the bag. Mitch said, "What you doing?"

"Making sure," said Sullivan.

"Did you ask the man permission?" asked Mitch. Sullivan looked up at Anders. Asked if he minded. The Cossack shook his head, said, "Be my guest."

They all watched Sullivan sift through the dirty underwear and socks. He grimaced, wiped his hands on his jeans. Mitch offered him a pair of latex gloves.

"Got any seps?" asked Mitch. Anders looked confused. "Separatees. Guys you need to stay away from or need to stay away from you." Anders shook his head.

"Load him up," said Mitch. Sullivan put him in the back of the Explorer.

"You guys drop Marci off at the courthouse," said Pete. "I've gotta get home."

"Nice," said Marci.

Mitch asked, "You want to drive?" She shot him a look and climbed into the passenger seat of the truck.

Sullivan said, "Thanks for coming out. That was awesome."

Marci eased the seat back and closed her eyes. "Try a different word. You owe me."

20

Big Maggie's house was big. It was also full. She didn't run a sanctioned halfway house and she wasn't registered anywhere as a foster mother, the state never would have gone for either, but she did fill an important role in the neighborhood and her boys, often as not, made it out of the hood eventually.

She relied on a combination of positive reinforcement, good food, and respect for elders to keep order in the house. There were clear rules for everyone who stayed with her, home by nine, nothing sharp or explosive, no smoking inside, and absolutely no Ho's. Break those rules and you were out. There were other rules too, and violations had their own special consequences a Catholic might recognize as penance and then be offended by the boys chanting Hail Maggie's.

The city left her alone because she never caused any trouble and there were more than a couple of officers who dropped boys off to her instead of taking them up to county.

Not everyone who stayed with her made it. You could take a boy off the street easy but taking the street off a boy? That took some doing and, according to Big Maggie, a whole lot of prayer.

She didn't ask how those prayers were answered. "If there's food on the table you eat it. You don't ask what it is or where it came from. There's kids starving over on Pearl and Eagle, you want that I scrape up your plate and run it over there?"

Lonnie was one of her first boys and she was proud of him. He'd spent plenty of time in jail, sure, but he never broke her rules. He'd gotten his GED inside and then learned accounting. They called it accounting, really it was how to balance a checkbook, but that was a talent Big Maggie hadn't picked up and she relied on Lonnie to tell her what was what.

What was what right now was being late on the electric. Lonnie said, "You got to pay these bills when they come in."

It was late and he was at the dining room table with bills and statements and napkins spread out all over the place. She plodded in with a mug of tea and dropped into a chair across from him.

"I got to have you around."

He said, "I got to have a job or my P.O. is going to put me back in." He was thinking about Jet. The Hummer, the nuts, and bottled water. They dropped him off before doing the wet-work but he knew what was going on. And he knew that the suit Wiggins had on cost more money than he'd ever had at one time.

"You thinking about that white boy?" she asked.

"Naw. I was thinking about Wiggins." She snorted at him. "What? I was thinking about the white boy before that, but not when you were asking."

"That way is trouble. You smarter than that." He was, but there was also a lot of money to be made working for people like Jet. There had to be a way and he said as much.

"Don't you fill your head with greed and lusts of the world, you hear me?" She actually pointed a finger at him.

"It's food money."

"No." She was firm there, if nowhere else. "Did you see his eyes? He's king of Babylon. Lord's gonna judge him harsh. You'll see."

Lonnie did see. A whole lot of money that could be his if he played it right. Trick was figuring it out when playing right meant doing wrong.

21

Mitch got home just before midnight. The lights were off and the driveway was empty. He dropped his bag by the door and walked through the dark to the kitchen. Grabbed a beer from the fridge and popped the cap off.

He stood in the living room and flicked through the channels on the TV while he drank. He tried to make a story out of the bits of dialogue he caught between switching.

He wandered upstairs and emptied his pockets. Badge on the dresser, gun on the night stand. He looked over at the empty dog bed. Probably should get rid of that.

He stood for a minute having the late night debate about brushing his teeth. Finally decided he should and then had second thoughts halfway through but didn't want to waste the toothpaste.

There was a time he would have washed up and changed into sweats. Now he just stripped down and climbed into the bed. The right side of the bed. Where the mattress was worn out.

22

Kurt Cunningham started every morning the same way. He polished his shield. There was not another FBI agent in the world who had a shinier badge and that was saying something. He followed that routine with the dedication you'd expect from an aging professional.

He called Gaff on his cell. Asked if there were any breaks. "No breaks, Kurt." Wondered if they could meet at 7:30. "I'll be at the office around 9. Why don't you stop in 11:30 or so and we can get lunch?" Kurt said, "See you at 9."

He had to find a way to break this case. For years he had been trying to bring down David Rask and for years the crafty old fox had out foxed him. Kurt could draw a dotted line between Rask the father and a dozen illegal enterprises running the gamut between smuggling, stolen goods, and human trafficking, but was never able to get the evidence he needed to connect the dots.

Rask was wealthy, but his on-paper wealth all appeared legitimate on that paper. He made a lot of money from his shipping business and Kurt couldn't figure out how he got his cut from the illegal activities. Kurt had been absolutely convinced he had him when Rask started his latest venture, an expansion of his self-storage line into cyberspace. But RaskBox, "on the ground and in the cloud," was clean. Squeaky clean. And everybody was using it.

There was a Russian connection. Ukrainian, actually, but Kurt was old school and the former Eastern Bloc was still all Russia to him. Problem was, the Ukrainian gangsters looked like investors, not partners.

At 8:53 Kurt climbed out of his tinted Taurus, nearly as shiny as his badge, and went into the courthouse. By 8:58 he was in the reception area of the United States Attorney's Office. It wasn't much, three chairs and an old copy of Cosmo, but it was as far as he could get until Terry Gaff arrived at 9:16 and signed him in.

"I want to look at the Russians again," said Kurt.

"They're Ukrainian."

"Get me a subpoena."

Terry set his leather messenger bag down on the floor next to his desk and sat. "Why don't you go after the son? Maybe you can get something, make a deal."

Kurt said, "I don't want a deal. I want to put David Rask away for life."

Gaff drained his travel mug. "I can't get you a subpoena. You don't have anything even close to P.C. Go after the boy. James?"

Kurt nodded. "He goes by Jet."

Gaff said, "What else do you know?"

Kurt smiled. "I know I got a guy inside."

Gaff didn't like that. "Anybody else know about it?"

"No need to share that."

"Ever heard of de-confliction?" asked Gaff. "You don't want your source compromised."

"He's cool." Kurt hadn't thought about that. Nobody'd mess with his investigation though. Besides, David was the big fish. Who cared about Jet?

23

The white Hummer with chrome spinners turned right off of Montague onto a private drive with a security gate. The gate was permanently open but still impressive. The truck followed the drive as it meandered through a grove of birch and out across an expanse of carefully tended sod sprinkled with shrubberies and flower gardens. They parked at the foot of a staircase leading up to an entrance terrace.

Wiggins got out of the front passenger door and opened the back door for Jet. Jet looked sharp this morning in pressed khakis and a button down shirt. Trey slid over to get out and Jet shook his head. Told him to get out on his own side.

Jet led the way to the front door, his boys a discreet distance behind. Trey said, "I'm not sure how much longer I can stand this." Wiggins told him to be cool. "But he's pissing me off." Wiggins nodded, understood, even understood if Trey wanted to walk away from the payday 'cause he was so tired of being pissed on.

Jet waited for the men at the door. They were cool, and when the Butler opened the door, they were gracious guests.

The Butler said, "Good morning, Master Jet. So good to see you. Your father is expecting you on the back veranda." He spoke with a faux accent that bordered between Scottish, East End London, and Australian.

"Thank you, Dear Chap," said Jet. "I can find my way. See if you can rustle up some chow for my men."

"Of course, Sir." He gestured to Wiggins and Trey. "This way."

Jet went off in the opposite direction through the immaculate and decadent mansion. He stepped through glass doors between the atrium and the veranda and spotted his father and Ginger eating fruit and eggs at a table near the swimming pool. They looked comfortable and were actually holding hands. Made Jet feel a little nauseous.

Ginger waved, parted her lips slightly and Jet thought he saw her tongue flick out just a bit. They were full lips set on a perfect face framed by naturally blond hair and Jet felt his face flush. David Rask turned from Ginger at the motion and faced Jet. He stood, embraced his son. "James, welcome."

"Jet."

"Hi, Jimmy," said Ginger.

"Shut up, Ginger," said Jet.

"Don't talk to your mother like that," said David.

"She's not my mother." Jet dropped into an empty chair, furious that he'd been reduced to a little boy in a matter of seconds. It was his father's talent. Ginger licked her lips, glanced brazenly at Jet as David leaned in for a kiss before sitting back down.

"Have something to eat, Jimmy." Ginger passed him a tray.

"I'm not hungry," said Jet. He popped some grapes then turned to his father. "There's been more than the usual number of problems this week."

"I know."

Jet said, "I had to replace Milton."

"Good. He was a punk." David sipped his coffee. "Imagined himself that guy from Pulp Fiction. What was it, Marco?"

Ginger said, "Mauricio."

David shook his head. "No, not Mauricio. Mickey? Montoya? Something like that."

"Mauricio." Ginger bit at some toast. A crumb stuck to the corner of her mouth and Jet couldn't look away.

David gave up. "Whatever. What did you do with Milton?"

"Put him down. DOA in hell."

Ginger giggled, rested her hand on Jet's leg under the table. David shook his head, said, "Jim, you've got to be more careful. That sort of thing brings on a lot of heat."

Jet was fired up, from his father's condescension and Ginger's hand. "Want to talk about heat? Let's talk about your friend Raj and the Feds."

David's face darkened. "Raj told me about your visit. You can't treat our partners like that."

Jet said, "He was holding out on us."

"And now he hates us."

"Good," said Jet. "Let him hate. We have our money. Who cares?"

"I CARE!" roared David, slamming his fist down on the table. Ginger jumped, then purred. "Raj has been good. If he has a problem, it's a real problem. We could have worked through it, but now? Who knows what he'll do."

David stared at his son. Jet kept the stare just as long as he dared then looked down at the table. He tried to cover by taking part of a donut.

"Raj knows things." David looked out over the pool, the expanse of lawn that stretched acres to a distant tree line. "He could hurt us."

"Want me to take him out too?" asked Jet.

"No, Jimmy. You aren't listening to me." David wiped his mouth with a cloth napkin. "You need to slow down. Stop acting like a street thug. I taught you better than this."

David stood. "I need to get to the office and take care of this. I want you to get out of town for a while. Let things settle a bit."

Jet said, "No way. I've got a club to manage and a crew to run. I've got plans."

David laughed. "Plans change."

Jet pouted. "I don't see why you're punishing me. Raj is the one with all the heat."

"Only because they haven't caught up to you yet," said David. "You never know what might happen and if they tie last night to you, put together your visits to his shop?" David shook his head. Jet started to speak but David held up a finger. "I'm tired of having to think for you. Of cleaning up after you. Take a break. Cool off. I'm not going to jail for your mistakes."

"I won't let you go to jail," said Jet. "Let me take care of Raj."

"I'll take care of Raj," said David. "You've done enough damage already."

Ginger tilted her head. "Poor Jimmy."

"Shut up, Ginger," said Jet.

David fumed. "Don't"- he stopped. Shook his head and stormed off. Jet and Ginger listened to doors slamming in the distance. Then it was quiet. Except for the birds. Jet took another grape.

"So, you sticking around for a little while?" asked Ginger.

"Wasn't planning to, why?"

She unzipped her sweatshirt and stretched. Jet watched her show, said, "of course, plans change." Ginger moaned softly. "And anything could happen."

She got up from her chair and went to Jet. He pushed dishes and platters out of the way. Shoved her onto the table. "And it's Marcellus. How can you be so stupid and still breathe?"

24

Mitch typed furiously at his computer with both index fingers. Pete was on E-bay looking at canoes.

Pete said, "So." Mitch didn't look up, "I'm working."

Pete continued, "Patti and I are having a barbeque this weekend. Few steaks, few beers, few friends. Good times. You want to come?"

Mitch kept typing. Pete said, "It'll be fun." No response. "Beers?" Still nothing. "Steaks?" Pete turned in his chair and looked across the room. "Mitch?"

"I'm busy."

"Take a break," said Pete. "Talk to me."

"I'm talking about your party."

"You're a big fat liar," said Pete. "I didn't even say when it was."

"You said this weekend," said Mitch. He looked up. "And I don't want to meet her."

"I'm talking about a cookout and you make me sound like a pimp," said Pete.

"You are a pimp," said Mitch. "Do you have any female friends left that I haven't spent an afternoon of awkward silence with?"

"Ouch." Pete put his hand over his heart. "That hurts, right here."

"I don't have time for this." Mitch started typing again.

"Dude, I'm the one that's supposed to be the old fuddy duddy."

Mitch looked over again. "Fuddy duddy?"

Pete said, "Yeah, that's what I said. I'm home early every night with the kid because my wife is starved for adult conversation and if I'm five minutes late she's discussing Maury Povich re-runs with the goldfish and I get cooking utensils thrown at me. You, on the other hand, are not bound by the laws of 'small baby living in your house-hood' and are free to do what you like BUT you go home early and don't socialize on the weekend. Fuddy duddy."

Venus and Chuck walked in with take-out coffee. Mitch said, "You're a jerk sometimes, Petersen."

"All I'm saying is that when you've got a chance to enjoy an afternoon with some friends and the company of a nice young lady, I don't understand why you don't take it."

Venus said, "Here's your coffee, Pete." He ignored her.

Mitch said, "I'll tell you why. It's excruciating. It's a waste of my Saturday. The conversation is always the same -- So, you wear a gun to work, huh? WOW."

"It's been 5 years. You need to get out there."

Mitch pushed back from his desk. "You think I don't know that? Every girl you introduce me to is in lust with the badge. You know how long those relationships last? One horrific night, if I'm lucky. They don't want this life. They don't have any idea what it's like to be attached to us. You want me to be some super stud that closes down the clubs every night and then bangs all of your wife's friends for you but NEWS FLASH, PETE. That ain't me."

"Come on, that's not what I meant," said Pete.

"Yeah?" Mitch stared hard. "It's what you said." He grabbed his ID badge from the computer. "I'm going for a run."

Pete said, "Hey, Mitch"-

Mitch cut him off, "I'm just going for a run. Don't worry about it." He pushed out past Venus and Chuck. They watched him go and then stared at Pete.

"What?"

Chuck snickered. "I didn't say anything."

Venus said, "Next time I say 'here's your coffee,' why don't you shut up and take it?" Pete took the coffee, said thanks.

Sipped at it, then said, "He's a monk."

Chuck said, "I thought he was a fuddy duddy." Venus laughed. Asked, "What got you guys started again, anyway?"

"Party at my place," said Pete. "Cookout. Beers, steaks."

Chuck said, "Ho's."

"No ho's," said Pete. "Thought I'd invite some girls from the clerk's office. See if they could get the new girl to come. What's her name?"

"Ginny," said Venus.

"Yeah, Ginny. Jenny?" asked Pete.

Venus was sure. "Ginny."

Chuck asked, "There going to be balloons and clown at this one too?"

Pete leaned back in his chair. "No, no, my good man. See, kids? They only have birthdays once a year. Not every other weekend."

"That's your plan?" asked Venus? "Invite some people so they'll invite some people so that maybe Mitch will talk to someone that he already sees every day? How did you even get married in the first place?"

The phone rang. Pete ignored it, gave Venus a hurt look. Chuck said, "I bought the coffee."

Venus frowned then answered the phone on her desk. "Task force." She smiled. "Tim, what do you have?" She nodded, looked around the office. "Me and Chuck. Mitch is out for a run, hold on a sec."

She looked over at Pete. "Can you come out and play or do you have to run home?"

Pete said, "I'm good." Venus went back to the phone, said, "Pete's okay too, but he has to stop by Costco to pick up some diapers and formula."

She grinned. "That's perfect. We'll meet you in the Costco parking lot in 20."

Chuck laughed. Pete gave her the finger.

Venus said, "It's hot. Brandt is hiding out Southside with a ho." She looked at Pete. He shook his head.

Chuck said, "The kid with the shotgun from last week?" and she nodded. "He's wired in with Rask, just like Trey."

They were already moving, vesting up, pulling long arms from the vault. Venus left a sticky note on Mitch's computer and they were gone. 10 minutes later the automatic lights shut off leaving their unfinished coffee in the dark.

25

Lonnie pushed one of those warehouse club flat carts between aisles of soup and boxed mashed potatoes. Shopping like this made him feel like a normal person. Oh, how about some animal crackers? "And why yes, I'll get an oversized triple pack of Captain Crunch."

He'd be lying if said he'd never been tempted to walk away with the cash money that Big Maggie gave him to cover the groceries, but a few hundred in hand wouldn't last that long and then where would he go?

At the checkout, the girl tried to give him a hard time because the membership card wasn't his, it was Big Maggie's. He thought the real reason was because she wanted to hassle a brother. He told her that Big Maggie was outside in the car. She said that Maggie O'Donnell could come on in and buy the stuff herself. She gave Lonnie that, "You found this card on the street, didn't you?" look.

He explained about Maggie's knees, about how she couldn't get around. The girl nodded, gave her best mmhmm, and then pointed to the wheel chair carts. Lonnie resorted to the big guns, I do this for her all the time. The girl switched looks to, "I bet you stole Maggie's purse."

The front end manager came over. Wanted to know what the problem was. The girl explained. Lonnie waited patiently, figured it was a good idea to not talk. The front end manager looked at the card, the groceries, then at Lonnie. Asked if he was part of a church group. He said, "No, ma'am."

The checker and the front end manager conferred for a minute, Lonnie heard something about no beer and real groceries and don't be dumb. The front end manager walked away and the girl took his money.

At the exit, he had to wait while the kid who didn't get the job as a square badge rent-a-cop checked off every item on the cart against the receipt. He was going to double check but there was a long line waiting to leave and the front end manager came over and told him to move it along. Lonnie asked if they were hiring but they weren't.

He loaded up Big Maggie's old Caprice. The kind with the big trunk and Corvette motor. She sat in the driver's seat reading about what James, the brother of Jesus, had to say on the subject of making long term plans. He climbed in beside her.

"Here's your change." She smiled at him and took it, said she loved how he always came back with the right change and just what was on the list.

"I got animal crackers," he said. She didn't care. "And they aren't hiring."

"You really going to get a job?" she asked.

"P.O. says I need to."

"That's not new."

He watched an Explorer with tinted windows pull into the lot. Cops. Had a bad moment when he wanted to jump out and run. Realized they weren't there for him. It was a good feeling. "I want to make it work this time."

26

The marshals rolled up on the collection of tinted and battered cars in the far corner of the Costco lot. There was the usual meet and greet and then Tim Churchill, the man from the phone call, got down to business. He was a state parole officer, assigned to the fugitive recovery office, and Brandt had been on his list for a long time.

The group of officers, a mixed force of state and city cops with the three marshals, gathered around the trunk of his car to get the skinny.

Tim said, "Here's the skinny. Brandt, Michael -- six one, two hundred, short black hair, yellowish brown eyes, yesterday was his 32nd birthday."

"So he's a cancer," said Pete. It didn't go over as well as he'd hoped and Venus elbowed him. Hard.

"Current warrant is failure to report. Ever. He's been out over 2 years and didn't make a single meeting with his P.O."

Venus asked, "What's the underlying?"

Tim smiled at her. She smiled back. "He was originally picked up for armed robbery. State BCI thought he was the guy in string of about 50 convenience store hold-ups including two murders but one of their witnesses died and the defense agreed to a deal so it never went to trial. He's been out of the state since he left prison, keeping a low profile until a couple of weeks ago when he came back here. Not really sure what he's into now, or why he's suddenly back in the area. It may be tied to Rask but we don't know, last week could have been a fluke."

Tim laid out the plan. Handed out wanted posters with Brandt's yellow eyes scowling out at them. Pete checked his watch.

Tim said, "The CI says she saw him at Booty Island a couple of nights ago with her former best friend. Said the two of them have been staying in, getting take-out and doing all kinds of nasty ever since."

27

They did a drive-by of 14373, a run-down single family that had been converted into apartments when folks thought this end of the city might get redeveloped as the new hip. The Scotch bars were gone, the brew pubs were gone, the book stores were gone, but the houses hadn't fallen down yet and there were no shortage of people who preferred a cheap roof to the street.

This particular house had a porch with an oven on it. Old clothes were piled everywhere, even down the walkway to the sidewalk. A few broken toys rounded things out and they were big ones, like a Fischer-Price slide and a pair of Sit-n-Spins.

The task force cars parked a few houses down. Tim keyed his radio and everybody bailed. The rear team ran through the narrow space between the house and its neighbor, cleared the back, then set up. When they were ready, the entry team walked down to the target house.

They moved onto the porch and Tim tried the door. It was actually locked. They heard a TV through the wall. Tim tried the door again, harder, and it popped open.

They crowded into the dark and musty entry hallway. A staircase rose along the left wall and they took it. Two officers stayed behind and covered the downstairs apartments with guns drawn, badges dangling from neck chains, and everybody listening to the TV.

The upstairs landing was crowded and exposed. The cops shifted nervously. Tim pounded on the door, announced "POLICE," and waited. He pounded again. Nothing. Tried the door but it was secured.

Chuck pushed up to the door. He put a peephole scope to the door and looked inside. "Food on the table. No people. Kitchen to left, hallway to right."

Tim said, "Warrant is for this address. Can you get in or do we need the ram?"

Chuck took out a Visa credit card and slid it along the jam. The latch slipped free. He rolled along the wall, out of the way, and Tim shoved in with Venus on his heels.

The cops poured through, guns up, splitting off to cover the apartment. Tim and the marshals cleared the dining room and started on the hall. First door was a bathroom, Venus moved to the next.

Kid's bedroom, different kind of messy than the rest of the apartment. Tim moved ahead to the last door, threw it open, went right while Chuck went left. Venus covered from the hallway.

Two heads were visible behind the bed. Tim shouted, "Show your hands." A 20 something black female stood up in a stained t-shirt. Told Tim to get out of her house. He demanded to see hands again. The second head popped up, belonged to a filthy little boy, about 10, in Wolverine underpants.

Chuck cleared the room. The woman, Chastidy, kept screaming at him to get out. Tim shouted over her, asked about Brandt. She ran out of steam. Tim said, "We have a warrant. You want us to leave? Tell me where Brandt is."

Chastidy was calmer. "If that warrant don't have my name on it you need to get out. I know my rights."

Tim said, "It doesn't work that way." Pete stuck his head in, said the back was clear. Chastidy started up again, said, "I told you he wasn't here."

She wanted pants and Tim told her she could have them, as soon she gave up Brandt. She wouldn't. "Toss it," said Tim.

"You can't do that," said Chastidy. The boy cowered beside her.

"We can and we will," said Tim. "You don't want that? Tell me where he is."

"I don't know," she said. Tim told her that wasn't good enough. That it was time to inventory the place. "I really don't know." Chuck believed her. Tossed her a pair of sweat pants.

They moved the party to the big room, put her in a chair. Tim sat opposite. She pouted and he waited. The boy squatted in a corner, watching as the cops went through the mass of clothes, garbage, and moldy furniture.

Tim asked, "When did he leave?"

"Maybe an hour ago," she said. Tim wanted to know where he went. She said, "I don't know. They just came and got him."

Tim and Pete exchanged glances. Tim asked who and she said, "I don't know. They just came in, sat right there while he got ready, and then left."

They waited. She looked around, couldn't take it anymore. "He didn't want to go. He wanted to stay with me. They made him go. I didn't like them, they scared me."

Venus moved to the corner and talked with the boy. A couple of the task force guys were pointing at things on the fridge.

"What are they doing over there? Get away from my fridge." She looked around. "Devron, get over here. Don't talk to her, she's a bad woman."

The boy ignored her. Led Venus back down the hall to the bedroom. One of the cops brought a picture over to the table, pulled off the fridge. It was Chastidy draped on Brandt at a club.

"Where's this?" asked Tim. She didn't know. "See? This is what I mean. You aren't helping. We're going to be here a while." She started to get up but the cop who brought the picture put his hand on her shoulder.

Tim said, "He's a wanted fugitive. What you're doing now is called aiding and abetting." She gave him her best "so what?" look. "That's five years."

She watched Devron and Venus go down the hall. "Where are they going?"

Tim said, "You should be more worried about where you're going." She tried on disdainful. Didn't quite pull it off.

Venus called from down the hall. Tim got up and Pete took his seat, said, "Hi, Chastidy. I'm Pete."

She didn't know what to make of that, or the hand he extended. She took it, shook. He smiled at her. She tried on confused and that suited her much better than disdainful had.

Pete said, "Look, I know you're worried about Michael, but don't be. We'll find him." She just looked at him. "See, I'm a marshal. That's what we do. Find people."

She said, "You're a marshal? I thought you all was cops."

Pete showed her his badge. "I should tell you, I'm very good at what I do." She said she was happy for him.

Tim came back from the bedroom. Dropped a 9mm on the table. That got her attention. "How about you stand up and put your hands behind your back?"

She stared at it, like it was going to go off. "It's not mine."

Tim said, "You're the only one here."

She shook her head. "It's Mike's. Not mine."

Pete said, "Not too smart to take off without his gun. Leaves you stuck with it, so to speak." She said it again, that it wasn't hers. "Problem with that," said Pete, "Is that he's not here and you are. The DA isn't going to be able to pin it on him. You can't be in possession unless you actually have it, like you do right now."

Chuck said, "The law is kind of funny like that."

She was worried. First time since they barged in. Tim got in her face, "Where's Brandt?"

She tried on hate and it was a perfect match. But it was too late and she said, "All I have is a number." Pete smiled at her. Slid his phone across the table.

28

Mitch felt better after the run and took advantage of the peace and quiet to finish his report. Until his cell rang. It was Pete, "I've got a number for you."

Mitch switched applications. "Go." Pete gave him the number and he punched it in. "Comes back to Gorlock Telco. Mean anything to you?" He heard Pete asking, heard Chuck answer but couldn't make it out.

Pete said, "Chuck says it's what Action Johnson uses." Mitch didn't know what that was. "I didn't either. Chuckles says it's an app that converts your conversation to packages and VOIPs them over the internet. No minutes."

"Or phone to track," said Mitch. "Looks like you guys are in for a long afternoon."

Chuck got on the line. "It's not a dead end. Go over to my desk." Mitch did. It was a mess. "There should be a stack of tan folders just to the left of my phone." There was. "Behind them is a copy of Muscle and Fitness."

Mitch picked up a copy of Wired. Said so. Chuck said, "Try the stack on your other left."

Sure enough, on the other left was the right magazine and a stack of papers. "Third or fourth down is the chief's memo about Friday dress code." Mitch pulled it out. "At the bottom is a purple sticky with a phone number."

Mitch read it off. Chuck said, "Sure. That's Scott Molson over at ESU. Call him and give him the number. Tell him it's an Action Johnson spoof."

Mitch repeated it back. "Why aren't you calling?" Chuck laughed and hung up. Mitch said, "No really, why aren't you calling?"

29

Lonnie was unloading the groceries from Big Maggie's car when Wiggins stopped by. He wasn't in the Hummer. He was driving a Benz.

Lonnie asked what brought him out of the slum. Wiggins laughed. "Wanted to say hello to Big Maggie." Lonnie nodded. "And talk to you."

Lonnie said, "Grab something and come on in. She'll be glad to see you."

They walked into the house. A half dozen young ne'er do wells were cleaning. Small price to pay for a safe bed and good cooking, if you asked any of them. Wiggins didn't. "Maggie? You home?"

She lumbered around the corner to see him. A smile lit up her face and she pulled Wiggins in tight. "So good to see one of my boys. You stopping to chat or need a place to stay?"

"Just saying Hi." He looked around. "You got a full house?" She shrugged. "Lot of food."

"Gets expensive," she said, looking at his suit. He flashed her a quick smile and then handed over a small wad of bills. She thanked him and tucked them away where no man would ever go searching.

Wiggins sat down at the kitchen table with Big Maggie and they chatted while Lonnie brought in the rest of the food. When he was done, Wiggins stood and said good bye. Lonnie walked him out.

Wiggins said, "So you thought about working for Jet?" Lonnie had. Quite a bit.

"I need a real job."

"It's better than a real job. More pay, less work." Wiggins smiled. Lonnie knew that. It was tempting.

"I'm going straight."

Wiggins laughed at him. "Man, nobody does that any more. Nobody even says that." Lonnie shrugged. Wiggins moved close, conspiratorial like, said, "Jet liked you. I could put in a good word."

Lonnie looked away. Wiggins shook his head. "You really are getting out of the game, aren't you?"

"Staying here," said Lonnie, "It changes a man."

"I stayed here plenty, still me," said Wiggins.

"I'm talking about now. Grown up." He looked back at the house. "I really appreciate the offer. I just like being able to go to sleep and not have to worry about being woken up in the middle of the night with a gun in my face."

Wiggins understood that. He offered his hand and it became a quick bro hug. "If you change your mind, come on by the club."

Lonnie watched him leave in the fancy car. Thought about the roll of bills he'd tossed so casually.

30

Mitch slipped into the OPS squad room. It was a ghost town, just a pair of DUSMs in the far corner and The Old Man in Steve's office shooting the breeze.

Mitch went over. "Afternoon, Chief," said Mitch to the old guy who was actually only about 53. "Steve." They asked what was up. "Got a task force case running all over town. Wondered if you could cut Sullivan loose."

Steve said, "He's up in court but you can have him when he's done."

Chief said, "He's been yapping about that arrest last night. How'd he do?"

"Good. Kid's a natural. Has the instinct. I want to see him in an actual pursuit."

Steve shook his head. "Don't get him too spun up. You know how these kids are. You give them some street time and all of a sudden it's 'nothing but warrants.' Can't get them to do anything. They go all man hunter."

"You were quite the man hunter in your day."

"You'll grow up eventually," said Steve.

Chief said, "Not Mitch. He'll be chasing bandits with a walker before you get him off the street."

Steve said, "I don't know, tell a guy he doesn't have to get up at 3 am, can be home for dinner most of the time and you'll give him a pay raise, how do you say no?"

Chief said, "That reminds me. Career board met last week and the promotion list is coming out on Friday."

Mitch said, "Don't worry. I'm not ready to sleep in yet. And being home for dinner is not on my bucket list."

"Just saying check your email when it comes out." Mitch wanted to know why but his phone rang. It was Molson with a trace on the Action Johnson phone.

"Have Sullivan call me when he's free," said Mitch.

Chief said, "What's Rodriguez doing over there?" Steve glanced at the corner, didn't look like Rodriquez was doing anything. Suggested maybe he was going up to court to relieve Sullivan. Chief thought that was a good idea. Said he'd send Sullivan over to the warrants office.

Mitch took off, already on another call.

Steve turned to the chief. "Who's getting promoted?"

31

Pete lounged on the chair across from Chastidy. She was done hating and was now resigned to the home invasion. Tim paced. Everybody else was waiting outside.

Hip hop music blasted into the room. Ring tone. They found her phone. Caller id said "Fresh." Tim asked if it was Brandt. She nodded.

Pete said, "It's your play but I think she's cool." He looked at Chastidy, rested his hand on the 9mm and said, "You're cool, right?"

She was. Tim said, "Reel him in." She answered the phone.

"Hey, Baby." He wanted to know if she was okay, why had it taken so long to answer. She played with her hair. "I'm okay, just sleeping, couldn't find the phone is all."

She listened for a beat then asked, "Where are you? It sounds loud." He said, "Out, what of it?" She said, "I was just wondering is all, 'cause it's so loud. You coming back to get me?"

Pete nodded to her. She was doing great. She poured on the gas, said, "Momma's got some hot sauce for you." Her face dropped. "How late?" She darkened. "You at the club? It sounds like you at the club. You coming back late because you got a ho?"

Pete wanted to know what he said because she melted, got all sweet again, and those words were worth gold. She said, "Okay, I'm sorry baby. I'll see you."

She hung up the phone. Pete smiled at her. She took it, but felt cheap and didn't want to give it back. She looked down, mumbled something.

Tim said, "What?" and she shouted at him, "Booty Island."

32

Booty Island was Rio Agua Caliente before Jet bought it. Not much changed other than the name. It was the sort of place you went if you wanted to be wild but not crazy, or if you were mad at your parents. And had money for the cover charge.

It was a little after 2pm when the three task force cars pulled up on the street outside the club. Two cops ran to the back. Tim and the marshals went to the door. Club was closed but it swung open with a light touch.

The interior was dingy in daylight, the flashing neon palm trees and treasure chests were switched off and looked cheap and dusty. The walls were streaked with nicotine and grease, the floor was sticky underfoot, and the thug sweeping on the far side of the dance floor didn't seem too much into quality control.

They almost missed the other guy who sat in the admission booth working on a ledger. His Booty Island t-shirt was clean and tucked into pressed black jeans. He said, "We're closed," without looking up.

Pete scanned around, said "That's good. If you were open I'd say you were about to go out of business."

The dude looked up. Pete and Tim flashed their badges. He checked them out, said, "What do you want?"

Venus and Chuck walked by, checked out the dance floor, the rest of the club. Noticed a stairway leading upstairs. The guy in the booth looked like he wanted to say something. Pete said, "That depends, you wanted for anything?"

Kid shook his head.

"Got any dope back there? Weapons?" asked Pete. Kid shook his head again. "I'm just a hard working citizen. You know how it is."

Chuck had reached the man sweeping. Was talking to him while Venus covered the big room from near the stairs.

Pete said, "Sure do. Looks like some long division over there, you want to take a break?"

He sighed, shut the book. Came out of the cage. Pete asked what his name was. Said it was Carlos. Said, "You're going to have to give me something, I have no idea why you're here."

"Sure thing," said Pete. "We want to talk to Brandt for a minute."

Carlos tried to pull a quick look over his shoulder, got caught. He said, "Who?"

Tim showed him a picture. "This guy."

"You probably know him as Cookie Monster," said Pete. No reaction. "No? What's he going by now?"

Carlos said, "I'm not sure why I would know that, Officer."

Tim said, "How about I just take a look around."

Carlos said no, said that they should probably just leave now, thank you, good bye. Nobody moved. He added, "We're closed, remember?"

Tim said, "Here's the thing. I've got a warrant for him and a solid lead that he's here. I can tear this place apart if I want to."

Carlos shook his head, put out his hands. "Why you doing this, man? You going to get me fired."

Pete said, "That would really suck for a hardworking man such as yourself." He put his hand on the kid's shoulder. "Why don't you just nod toward where he's hiding?"

Carlos said, "He's not hiding."

There was a noise on the stairs and Venus called out. She moved off-line, hand on her pistol, watching the landing up top.

"Who else is here?" asked Pete.

Carlos said, "What?" A big grin on his face. Pete pushed passed, set up with Venus. Brandt was on the stairs, talking into his cell. He looked just like the mug shot but in street clothes. He took a look at the cops and jumped the half flight over the rail and onto the dance floor.

Venus and Pete closed fast, screaming at him not to move, police, all of it. He sprinted toward the door. The sweeper brought his broom around on Chuck but he was ready and caught it, snapped it, and did some Kung Fu.

Tim wasn't so lucky. He was surprised when Carlos made a move and went down hard. Brandt jumped over the fighting men and out the front door, Venus on his heels. Pete was right behind but stopped to help Tim fight free. Then they were out too.

Chuck landed a couple of extra shots on the sweeper, noticed everybody was gone and ran for the door, stooping to pick up a lost phone on his way.

Carlos was just starting to push himself up when Chuck launched off his back and through the door into a mess.

Brandt had surprised the officer's outside and one of them panicked, used his pepper spray. It wasn't a good shot but left a cloud of vapor right at the entrance. It got everybody coming out, Chuck was late enough it wasn't too bad.

Brandt was down the street and turning into an alley by the time anyone was in a car and pursuing. The guys from around back heard the commotion and set off on foot.

Tim was furious but you couldn't tell, they were all spluttering from the spray. At the car Chuck pushed Venus out of the way. "Better let me drive."

33

Jet watched all the cops leave through the security monitors in his upstairs pad. He was giddy, slapped Wiggins on the back. They went downstairs.

The sweeper moaned but hadn't moved much. Carlos limped over when he saw the boss. "Sorry. I tried to get them out of here."

Jet waved it off. "Don't worry about it, you did good." He checked out the point where Brandt had jumped. Moved over to where Venus had been standing. Half ran through what had happened, big grin plastered on his face. Kept saying, "So cool."

Wiggins asked, "You okay, Boss?"

Jet said, "Yes. Did you see what happened?" They all had. "Those were marshals and they're looking for me."

Carlos said, "They were looking for Brandt." He trailed off at a look from Wiggins.

Jet walked toward the back, kicked at the sweeper and said, "Get this guy. We need to get out of here before they come back looking to hard time everybody."

34

The Explorer was booking, lights and sirens running. Mitch drove one handed, punched a number into his phone with the other. It kept not going through.

Sullivan was in the passenger seat, excited and terrified. "Try voice dialing."

Mitch looked at him, almost hit a car swerving to the side of the road. "Voice dialing?"

"Just give it to me, I'll dial for you." He closed his eyes for a second as the truck squeezed between two cars. When he opened them Mitch's phone was in his face. Mitch told him to get Pete. He did.

Mitch shouted into the phone, "Got some great news for you."

35

Pete was on Putnam Avenue, a few blocks from Booty Island. It wasn't as run down as some parts of the city, but it wasn't the home of the Ritz Galleria either.

He was on the phone. Said, "We could use some. Brandt got away."

Mitch said, "Not for long. ESU tracked the phone. We've got a location. I'm heading there now with Sullivan."

"Great. What do you have? We'll head over."

"5476 Putnam. I think that's down by Booty Island."

Pete said, "It is. That's where we lost him. He must still be hanging around." He looked around. Chuck asked, "What?" Pete said, "ESU puts Brandt at 5476 Putnam."

They heard a siren in the distance. "5476?" asked Chuck. Pete said yes. "Like that 5476?" Chuck pointed to the numbers on the door of consignment shop next to where they were parked.

The siren grew louder then cut out. The explorer came into view. "What's going on?" asked Pete.

Chuck said, "They aren't tracking Brandt anymore." Mitch and Sullivan jumped from the truck and ran up.

"You guys got here fast," said Mitch.

Chuck said, "You came to us." He held up the phone he'd picked up on the way out of the club. "He dropped this. You were tracking me."

"Who sprayed you guys?" asked Mitch. Venus gave him a look. He dropped it.

Tim shook his head. "Back to the girlfriend? Not sure what else we have."

Pete thought they might have better luck at Booty Island, but Tim had already sent marked units to scoop up the sweeper and Carlos and they'd found the place deserted.

"I mean from a stake out perspective," said Pete.

Chuck leaned over to Venus, said, "So should I suggest checking out the phone we recovered or let these guys stay out all night for no reason?"

"What did you find?" asked Venus.

"Nothing yet, haven't looked. But anybody using Action Johnson is geek enough to have an address book full of leads."

Venus pulled Mitch's arm, pointed to the phone. His eyes lit up. Chuck said, "Only thing, Boss. We don't have a warrant."

Mitch said, "Bandit dropped it during pursuit. I'd say it's fair game."

Chuck poked at the phone. "He's got a password." Sullivan moved over, looked over Chuck's shoulder. Suggested he try the bypass. Chuck scowled at him, said, "Great idea. I'll do that after I figure out how to tie my shoes."

Pete asked if anyone had cologne. "I smell like a burrito truck."

Sullivan said, "Stop wasting your chances. That phone will wipe when you get to the end."

Chuck turned, real slow. "Excuse me?"

Sullivan pressed on. "You got a laptop? Let's just break the door down."

Chuck, "Where did you find this kid, Mitch?" But he walked around to the back of the truck and opened up his gear bag. Took out a Dell Toughbook and collection of cables. "Go ahead, Mr. Wizard."

Mitch said, "No cologne."

Venus tossed Pete a bottle. "Try this, tough guy."

"Why do you carry cologne?" asked Pete.

"It's perfume. You'll like it."

He did, said, "Smells good." Looked at the bottle. "Daisy?" Sprayed some more.

Sullivan wanted to know if Backtrack 1789 was installed. Chuck just hit the icon. On the home screen. It booted, marshal's star as the new background. Sullivan opened the Krak-N app.

"Whoa, slow down. That'll wipe the phone," said Chuck.

Sullivan shook his head. "Not anymore. The 5 point 4 patch fixed that. We should be able to just"- and they were inside the phone. Chuck was impressed.

Mitch pushed over. "What's in there?"

Sullivan said, "All kinds of stuff." But he didn't know what to look for. Handed the reins back over to Chuck. Venus patted him on the shoulder, told him, "Good work." It was enough.

Pete sprayed more of the perfume.

Chuck said, "Looks like a full schedule." They went through the calendar. Tim stuffed a handful of Big League Chew into his mouth, copied the next appointment and address into his note book, and took off with the task force cops. "I'll call if we get anything."

The marshals kept at it. Dug up a few more appointments with addresses. "This one's in an hour and half," said Chuck.

Pete handed Venus back her now empty bottle of perfume. She frowned at him. "Regulators, let's ride," he said.

There was a bit of shifting around, Sullivan wanted to ride with Venus and nobody wanted to ride with Pete, the sweetest smelling deputy in the service.

36

Katherine Silver parked the U-Haul truck on the street. She still had furniture in the back. She needed to do something about that.

Her phone rang. It was Mark. She didn't want to talk to Mark. She'd moved away from New York to get away from Mark. She answered.

Mark wanted to know if she was okay, which she was and if she'd managed to get moved in yet, which she had not. "See, I'm worried about that because you haven't returned the rental truck yet and I'm still paying for it."

She'd forgotten he agreed to pay for her truck. A smile crossed her face. "So how about I come down there, help you finish unloading, and then I can return the truck for you." Smile gone.

"That's okay."

"Kate, you've got to return the truck." He used his passive-aggressive voice, the one that said, "I will take you to court because if we fight on the street I'll lose."

"I will," she said. "Good bye."

Katherine leaned against the truck. Then called Cindy. Offered to trade pizza and beer for a little help. She agreed.

37

Mitch drove while Pete watched the world go by. The good time radio was on, turned low and playing something about love from the eighties.

"You end up putting in for that job in Billings?" asked Mitch.

Pete, caught off guard, "Why? Well, yeah. I mean, it's a long shot, but you know, a cabin by a lake?"

Mitch did know, but he didn't get it. "You'll have to learn how to build a bird house."

"That's what Patti said." Pete looked out the window, straight ahead. "It's Montana. Those jobs don't open up very often. You have to go after what you want, right?"

Mitch said, "I'm not judging."

"Sure you are," said Pete.

"Sorry." Mitch turned at the light. Tried to leave it back at the intersection and couldn't. "But Ops supervisor? You see what that did to Steve? He used to be one of us."

Pete had seen that. Thought about that. He didn't want to be a supervisor here. "We're talking about out West. It's a lighter load, different lifestyle. Horses, fishing, safe schools." Mitch shook his head. "Besides, there's like 40 applicants anyway. I'm not going to get it, everyone wants to go there."

"Not me," said Mitch. "Too cold. You ever even been there?"

Pete looked at his friend. "I'm not going to get it. Stop worrying."

"I'm not worried," said Mitch. "I just wondered if you put in."

Pete's phone rang. He took it. A bunch of "Oh really?" and "You're kidding," followed by, "We're rolling on the next stop now, that's probably good too."

He hung up, looked out the window. Mitch said, "So he was there but they missed him?"

"That's easy, a court monkey could figure that out. Impress me."

Mitch flexed his arm, put his bicep in Pete's face. Pete pushed it away. "Nice. The address was a Phone Depot. When Tim showed up the clerk puked all over, gave up Brandt, the new phone, and the bag of stuff."

"What bag of stuff?"

"He didn't know. It was a bag, had stuff in it. His job was to give it to the guy who asked for it, not look inside. Anyway, guess whose stuff it was?"

"Rask."

38

The marshals set up on the Metro platform. It was crowded, evening rush hour getting into full swing. Chuck and Mitch worked through the press of commuters while Venus and Chris Sullivan hung at the stairs.

"We sure this is the right place?" asked Chris.

"No," said Venus. "You never know. This could be a total waste of time. You strike out a lot in this business."

"But you keep trying?"

"Of course." She looked around, turned back to him. You can get shut out and shot down a hundred times but sooner or later you find the hole, make it through, get the guy."

"Is it worth it?"

She grinned. "Oh yeah. The catch is always worth the effort. And we always catch our man."

"Or woman?" asked Chris. He was going for double entendre but didn't pull it off. She snorted and looked away. Saw Brandt fifteen feet away. Their eyes locked.

He bolted and she was on him. Sullivan took a moment to shift gears. Mitch and Chuck heard her shouting, "Police." Brandt dodged, ran along the edge of the platform. He tripped, knocked a woman over the side.

She screamed over the announcement of an impending arrival. Everybody saw the train coming, everybody saw her on the tracks. The crowd of people too thick for Brandt to escape or for the marshals to reach the woman.

Brandt reached down and pulled her up. A few others joined in to help him. Then he was tackled from behind by Sullivan, Venus with him. Mitch shoved a hole in the crowd to work.

They cuffed him, searched, and Venus said, "What the?" when they found the wire. Mitch scratched his head, stood. Saw Kurt Cunningham and Robert Something-or-other pushing toward them at the far side of the platform.

Chuck said, "Guess we know why he came back to town. He's working for the FBI. Nobody saw Trey slip away from the platform, a bag of stuff slung over his shoulder. He descended the stairs and walked across the street, right in front of the black Explorer. He looked in at Pete. Pete looked out.

Trey pointed his finger, like a gun, grinned, and hopped into a white Hummer. "How did I not see that?" asked Pete, his heart pounding, image of his son orphaned burning his eyes.

39

Cindy pulled up behind the U-Haul. It looked like the one that had been parked at the courthouse all week, with the Indian and corn stalk mural on the side. The back was open and Katherine sat inside on her couch drinking a Red Bull. She tossed one to Cindy.

Two hours later they were at the kitchen table inside the house sharing a half broccoli half peperoni thin crust and washing it down with a domestic light. The U-Haul was safely returned and its contents were now mostly in the middle of the down stairs rooms.

"How are you going to get to work now?" asked Cindy. Good question. Cindy covered her mouth to keep the pizza in while she laughed. "You haven't thought about that."

Katherine said, "You have no idea how hard this has been for me." Cindy said, "Tell me," popped open a couple more beers, and pulled her leg up under her on the chair the way some women do.

So Katherine told her. About New York. About Mark. About her father's friend the chief judge of the district who got her the nomination. She was a mess. And funny. When the beer was gone they switched to wine.

40

It was after dark when Pete finally pulled into his driveway. He took a deep breath, then got out and pulled several bags of groceries from the back. The front door opened as he got close to the house, the doorway holding all five feet of Patti, a Guatemalan fireball fifteen years younger than Pete who had been waiting a long time for him to show up.

"Baby, you're home!" She ran out of the house barefoot, wearing boxers and a t-shirt stained with spit-up.

Pete asked, "How are you feeling?"

"Today was a good day," said Patti. "Except that my deadbeat husband never called to tell me he was going to be late." She slugged him. "Why don't you ever call?" It was a whine. "I was worried sick for you. Here I am, with your child, and nobody to take care of us and you are dead in the street."

Pete tried calm. "Easy, Honey. I'm not dead. We had a big case, it didn't go quite the way we expected but I didn't want to call and wake up the baby."

She said, "Oh. You are so sweet. How did I get so lucky?" But then the wind blew and she was angry again. "But Baby, why didn't you at least send me a text? I have been waiting for Mitch to call and tell me I can come visit you as soon as they get you out of emergency surgery."

Pete didn't have time to think. He went with, "Because Baby, we were busy on the case and this guy, he was a bad man. I needed to keep Mitch safe and if I was texting you he might be the one in the hospital." It seemed to be working. "I was just trying to keep everybody safe and happy. I didn't want you to be worried, I thought you might have been able to get in a little nap and if I called and woke you up during the fifteen minutes you get to yourself all day, well, I'd have felt terrible."

She kissed him. "Oh Baby, you are so wonderful. I love you."

He kissed her back. "I love you too, Baby." He tried for a bit more of the kissing but it was awkward with all of the grocery bags.

Patti pulled back, thoughtful. "But Baby?"

"Yes, Baby?"

"If it was really that dangerous," she slugged him hard, "What were you doing there? You promised me that after the baby was born you would stop doing this, stop with the dangerous cases but instead you are here, late, not calling, and breaking your promise working a dangerous case. You can't text because Mitch would go to the hospital?" Her hands were on her hips. "You think I am stupid? And what is that smell? Is that perfume on you?"

Pete said, "Yes. It's perfume. We were in a lot of places, got a lot of smells. Bad, awful smells. This is all Venus had."

Patti relaxed. "Venus was with you?" He told her that's what he'd been trying to say all along. "Well, why didn't you? I'm sorry to yell, Baby. It's a long day here without you. A woman gets to missing her man."

Patti walked toward the door, shaking all the right parts. Pete said, "Really?" She looked over her shoulder, said, "And a baby only sleeps for so long."

Pete rushed after her. "I'll drop these in the kitchen and be right there."

She smiled at him, said, "Okay." Then she got curious. "What's with the groceries?"

Pete said, "I was thinking, how do you feel about having some people over on Saturday?"

The booty shake stopped. "Here?" There was more and it wasn't nice. The best Pete could offer was, "It was Mitch's idea."

41

Steve walked over to Warrants in his suit. It wasn't very far from Ops to warrants physically, but he felt like he'd crossed the equator, moved into the dark side, something. It was a different world. He missed it.

Venus looked up when he came in. Greeted him. So did Chuck, but Pete kept working. Steve said, "Pete, I need you for magistrate court."

Pete said, "What?" Steve repeated himself. Pete said, "What?"

"Funny," said Steve. "Calendar starts at 2. You don't need to change out, just meet the guys in Silver's court room. You can cover the gallery."

"I really don't think that's a good idea, sort of wastes my talent."

"You're up on the rotation," said Steve. "See you at 2." Pete made a face, one of the mean kind. Steve said, "If you want, we can change that to 7 every morning. Sullivan would love your spot on the squad."

"Easy. I'll be there." Steve left. Pete stared after him for a beat, then turned on Chuck. "Thanks. Really appreciate it."

"Say what?" asked Chuck.

"You covering court for me like that," said Pete. "Real big of you."

"I'm not covering your court."

"Why not?" asked Pete.

"You still owe me from the last time I covered for you."

Pete tried again, "You know, I was just thinking that you are an amazing court deputy and since you are so much better at it than I am"-

Chuck cut him off. "Nobody is so much better at court."

Pete got pissy. "Alright, how about because I'm such a better investigator than you are?"

Chuck said, "I don't think today is going to work for me. Sorry."

Pete found some passion. "You don't know what it's like for me in there. All those people, the chairs, the tables, the formal language. Neck ties, lawyers. And that giant digital clock that ticks away my life. Tick. Tick. Tick." Pete grabbed a breath. "I can't do it. I'll go insane. Start busting caps."

Chuck, finished, "I'm gonna start busting caps. I'm not doing your court. Shut up already."

Pete swiveled his chair slightly. "Venus?"

She said, "Don't even start with me."

Pete kicked back. Crossed his arms. "Fine. Do either of you even know what I'm working on over here?"

Chuck, still annoyed, said, "Do tell, Sweet Pea." Venus chuckled, said she thought that was good enough it might stick.

"It's not going to stick," said Pete. "It's stupid. I don't have time for this. You know what? I'll do the stupid court and then I'll stay late and finish this stupid lead. You just sit over there surfing Amazon with your stupid grins and make-up nick names for the people who do the real work around here." He glared at Chuck.

Venus said, "Relax. He's got to get the subpoena request done so it can get to the judge before the end of the day."

"How does that help me?" asked Pete.

"Let it go," said Venus.

"Do you know what happens when I get home late every night?" asked Pete. Chuck suggested what he thought wasn't happening. Pete bit his head off, "Real freaking funny."

Venus said, "So maybe you should have a chat with her. Explain how things are, about how you have to take turns at work, like a big boy. Do your share of court."

"Hilarious." Pete turned back to his desk. Then spun around to look at them again. "You can't explain something to a woman who spends all day with a baby that doesn't talk and no adults anywhere. Do you understand the kind of mood swings she has?"

"Must be rough," said Chuck, "If they're anything like yours." Pete glared. "Take her out. Show her a good time."

Pete said, "You aren't even listening. I get home and she's in sweats pulling out her hair. The last thing in the world she wants to do is go somewhere."

"So stay in," said Chuck. "Give her some loving."

"Give her some..?" Pete shook his head. "You don't go there with a crazy woman."

Venus said, "You need to do something to get things worked out. Or make a side arrangement. You're a real pain in the ass to work with lately."

"Side arrangement?" Pete's lips moved a little bit, warming up while he figured out what to say. Wasn't worth the wait. "How'd we get from Chuck not helping out to me needing something on the side?"

Mitch walked in, caught the last. "You've got a side deal?"

"No," said Pete. Chuck and Venus both started to speak but he shushed them. "Steve came in needing help with court, Judge Silver. I've got to get this lead entered or we'll be late and HQ will be all over us. Again. But nobody seems to want to be a team player."

Mitch looked over at Chuck. "Still working on the LA subpoena?" He nodded. Venus just looked back at him. He smiled at her. "Fine. I'll do it."

Chuck said, "What?" Pete waved him off, said, "It's at 2. Didn't say how long."

Mitch asked, "Do I need to change?"

"Didn't say," said Pete. "Probably a good idea though, new judge and all."

Mitch turned to the door. Pete was back to himself, asked, "Think you can make the party this weekend?"

Mitch said, "Told you already, I don't feel like fighting off any more groupies."

"Fair enough," said Pete. "Just class, no cheap dates."

"No strangers that you met at the grocery store buying last minute stuff."

"What kind of friend do you think I am?" asked Pete. They all looked at him. "Okay. No strangers."

Venus said, "You're wasting your time with conditions. He'll find a loophole."

"Good point," said Mitch. "How about I just bring a date? Will that keep you from inviting someone I have to meet?"

"A date?" asked Chuck.

Pete said, "Sure. Bring a date. We'll sit next to you guys and watch the pigs fly by."

"I'm serious," said Mitch. "If I bring someone will you promise not to subject me to another round of the Matchmaking game?"

"Scout's honor," said Pete. "I won't invite anyone. But you show up alone and we'll never have this conversation again."

"Agreed," said Mitch. "But I want something better than Scout's Honor. Something binding."

Pete didn't follow. Mitch said, "New kid says you taught him to pinky-promise."

Mitch headed out, chuckling to himself and looking for his suit which, if he remembered correctly, was still in a locker somewhere down the hall.

Chuck asked, "What just happened there?"

"Pete got our boss to cover his court," said Venus. Pete nodded his head. "And tricked him into changing out." He nodded again. "Even though he didn't have to." Pete grinned. "And he said he was coming to the party with a date."

Dumbfounded. Then Chuck said, "I think Sharita and I will be able to make the party after all."

42

Kurt paced around the conference room in the United States Attorney's Office. It was crammed with charts, pictures, and dry erase boards covered with different colored lists and cross outs. The space was too small, the case too big, and the G-man was angry.

"Damn." Turn. Step, step, step. "Damn." Turn. Step, step, step.

Gaff looked up from an interview transcript. "We'll find something."

"We were close." Kurt stopped pacing. "Brandt was our in. He was on the edge of giving us something really good. I know it."

"So we'll get it another way," said Gaff.

"But no, the marshals ride in like a bunch of cowboys. All, Hey! Look at us! We put handcuffs on people and ruin investigations."

He started pacing, knocked over a stack of folders. "Like it takes more than five seconds to learn how to do that. We've put three years into this case."

"You knew he had an active warrant," said Gaff. "You knew it was a risk not telling anyone and you thought it was worth it."

"It was worth it," said Kurt, "Would have been. If they hadn't arrested him. And they went to the club! How are we supposed to get anyone in there now?"

Gaff shrugged. Can't argue with crazy.

Kurt said, "Freaking Kannenberg. That's the problem." He kept pacing. "Mitch Kannenberg is always the problem."

43

Katherine chewed on the tip of a pencil. She wasn't hungry, she was bored. She understood why so many judges got really good at golf. But she hated golf. One more reason why she didn't belong in the dark paneled office. Another was her bicycle which replaced the U-Haul until she got around to buying a car. And of course, what other judge had "Danger Danger" playing on her iPod?

Cindy stuck her head in. "Need anything else?"

Katherine said, "No. You heading home?"

"Out, actually," said Cindy. "It's 80s night at Gillian's."

"Sounds fun."

Cindy said, "You aren't like any other judge I've ever met, you know that?" She hesitated, then added, "A bunch of us are going. If you want to come."

Katherine thought about it. Cindy said, "No other judges, but some of the lawyers come, it wouldn't be like it was just" – she trailed off, unsure.

"Just common folk?" asked Katherine, laughing.

"I meant it wouldn't be just clerks and marshals."

"I was talking to a marshal over there the other night," said Katherine.

"Which one?"

"The scruffy one that walked into the table."

Cindy raised an eyebrow. "Mitch? I bet that was interesting."

Katherine looked through her. "Interesting is a good word."

Cindy started to go then stopped, said, "Girl to girl?" Got Katherine's attention. "Watch out for Ramon. He's a dog. Do NOT let him buy you a drink."

Katherine nodded. "Anyone else I should watch out for?"

Cindy said, "Depends on what you and Mitch were talking about."

44

Big Maggie didn't ever raise her voice. She'd speak quietly, maybe point every once in a while, and that was enough. That particular afternoon she stood outside one of the bedrooms in her house, packed with bunk beds and street kids cleaning up. And she pointed. Toward the door. Clarence, somewhere in the vicinity of age 17 and 130 pounds, got the message but didn't acknowledge it. A few of the other boys gathered around. Some were cleaner, some were younger, all of them shared Big Maggie's concern about the drugs he'd brought into the house.

One of them said, "You know the rules. This is your own dumb ass fault." That was one of the older ones, a boy working on his GED and responsible for running the yard crew.

Clarence ignored him, asked Big Maggie why. She said, "Lord says trying to learn up a fool makes you a fool."

Clarence said, "Doesn't he say something about the down trodden too?"

"He does," she said. "Says they need to get on up out of here. You get some of that humility, come on back."

He saw the looks of the other boys. They were right. He did know the rules. "Can I at least take my stuff?"

Big Maggie walked away. The boys would take care of him. She doubted Clarence would ever find his way back to her house, or any house for that matter. Boy was going to die on the street. Tragic, but nothing more she could do. Man's got to choose life for himself. That one chose meth and she had no patience for it. Rest of the brothers struggling and all.

She ambled down to her bedroom, the only private room in the house. She had a recliner set up where the wall sort of bumped out like a turret, let in a lot of light. A glass of ice tea sat on a coaster next to it. The room was remarkably feminine. Not that she wasn't, just that folks didn't think like that when they looked at her.

She heard the front door slam and watched Clarence mope away. She could see a couple of boys on the front lawn, seeing him off. She watched him stare long eyes of hate toward them all. Blaming the boys for turning him in, for being narcs when all he needed was a little fix. Boy needed to take responsibility for himself before he could get better, she reminded herself. He had to go. Like as not a few of the others would have shared in the stash, next thing she'd have her very own crack house and that was not what God wanted from her.

Lonnie walked down the path to the street, wearing a shirt and a tie. That boy was a success. He got it. She was very proud of him. Loved him even, like her own son. She smiled and offered up a prayer to the Almighty, asked that he keep that boy clean and please, oh please, get him a job.

45

Jet sat at the bar of Booty Island. Wiggins mixed drinks for the half dozen guys currently providing muscle. Jet called it a staff meeting. Said staff meetings were what made them successful, better than the other gangs. Jet was crazy.

Wiggins slid a bourbon martini to his boss. He'd been a bar tender one summer, after his first stretch, when he thought maybe going back to jail wasn't a good idea. It wasn't a bad job, but he didn't really care for regular hours and he could get just as much action by flashing his roll of bills as he ever did mixing drinks. He'd never mixed a bourbon martini before. Had to ask what it was when Jet told him to make one the first time. The Booty Island version was Jim Beam in a martini glass. He supposed in another place it might be Jack or even Jameson. If you could call a drink with bourbon a martini, why couldn't you make a bourbon martini without bourbon?

Jet was saying, "We're going to have to head out of town. But the club stays open, so a couple of you will be here. I don't plan to be gone long, but you know how the old man can be." They didn't. None of them knew their fathers. "So we'll do a rotation, maybe. Let everybody have some time up at the lake."

They liked that. "It'll be like a corporate retreat." They didn't know about those. Didn't matter to Jet. He liked this part of being the boss. They liked how he paid them. Didn't matter if they were making a run, bouncing the club, or shooting up a former partner. Or playing team building exercises by the lake.

Jet looked around. "Where's Brandt?" Everybody else looked around. Trey said, "Maybe he got picked up? I saw one of the marshals at the metro station."

Jet flew off his stool. "You saw a marshal and didn't tell me about it? After they chased us out of here?"

Trey leaned back. He was coming off a high and not enjoying the trip down. "Didn't realize it was a big deal. They weren't after me, didn't think we were connected."

"How could you not think that?" asked Jet.

"I had the bag and he ignored me." Trey looked for support from the crew. It sounded good to them.

Wiggins said, "I'll call around. See what happened."

Jet said, "Fine. We'll take Carlos."

Wiggins said, "You want me to stay and do the money?"

Jet shook his head. "No, you need to stay with me." He thought about the money. "Get somebody you can trust that knows how to add."

Wiggins made a note on a napkin and stuck it in his pocket. "When do we have to leave?"

Jet said, "I don't want to leave." Everybody drank, not sure what they were supposed to say. "I guess tonight. I'm sort of pushing things now with the old man." Again, nobody sympathized, nobody could relate.

46

Lonnie Perez did not get hired by the nice lady who managed the Burger King on Danforth. He also didn't get hired by anyplace else that had a sign out. He was bummed and a sweaty mess. He bought a coke at 7-Eleven and sat on the curb, wondered how understanding his P.O. would be. He really was trying.

Wiggins pulled in to fuel up his Benz. Spotted Lonnie and walked over, pointed to the tie, said, "How's life working for the man?"

Lonnie said, "Don't know. The man won't hire me."

Wiggins said, "I can get you in."

Lonnie knew he could. "You know I need a real job, got to pay taxes or the P.O. won't count it." Wiggins laughed. "This isn't about some spending money, it's about working."

Wiggins understood that. Then, curious, asked, "You good at math?"

Lonnie shrugged. "Guess so. I do Big Maggie's checkbook."

Wiggins nodded. "You want to work at Booty Island?"

"Jet's place?"

"He needs somebody to manage for a few days. Do a good job he'll probably keep you on." Wiggins looked out. "Guy does it now is skimming. Jet sees what's really coming in, could be bad. You think you could handle that?"

"Sort of a real job but with a little extra too?"

"Some extra to spread around." Wiggins looked back at Lonnie. "You'd have to keep him cut in while he's around or he'll knock you out, no matter what I say."

Lonnie said, "I get that. Jet doesn't know about it?"

"I'm sure he suspects, but what does he care? Man's a cake eater." Wiggins laughed. "And he eats it right out of my hand."

Lonnie stood up. "Who would I be working for? Him or you?" Wiggins asked if he had to be anywhere. Lonnie didn't. Wiggins gave him some cash, said to get a couple of grape slurpees and come back to the car.

Five minutes later they were riding in the Benz, slurping away the summer heat. Wiggins said, "Here's the deal. Jet is an idiot but he's loaded. Trick is figuring out where the money is. You're going to figure that out."

Lonnie nodded. Slurped. "Why hasn't the guy doing it now figured it out?"

"Because he's an idiot too. Happy with a few hundred a night in his pocket. No imagination." Wiggins turned onto Western and they headed downtown. "Or loyalty. Can't trust him to do it right or keep his mouth shut."

"You need an honest thief," said Lonnie.

"I need a brother," said Wiggins. "Jet trusts me, but that's because I don't push or ask the wrong things. Never make him suspicious. It's a good place to be, comfortable, but there's no future in it. I have plans that don't involve Jet." Lonnie waited. "But they do involve his money."

"So I work for Booty Island, according to my P.O.," said Lonnie. "And I work for Jet, according to him."

Wiggins nodded. "And you work with me so that you can do whatever you want the rest of your life."

"How much we talking?"

Wiggins didn't know. "I see him collect a hundred grand some weeks. I know a lot of it goes to his father, but not all. He's into things that the old man doesn't know about."

"And he's skimming too, right?"

"I taught him that." Wiggins pulled into the parking lot of a 24 hour pharmacy, couple blocks from Booty Island. "You want in on this?"

Lonnie enjoyed the last of his Slurpee. It was the best one he'd ever had. "I am most definitely in. When do I start?"

Wiggins grinned. "My brother, you start right now." He took out his cell phone, called Jet. Said, "I've got your new money man." Paused, said, "I'll bring him by. You've met him. It's Lonnie." Another pause. "Oh yeah, you can trust him. We're brothers."

Lonnie looked at the inside of the car. The leather. The chrome. It smelled wonderful. He could have a car like this. And not have to look over his back for the cops. Wiggins, still on the phone, said, "No, not real brothers. Remember? I told you about how I knew him."

Wiggins got off the phone. Handed Lonnie a $20. "Go in there and buy a can of mixed nuts. You give those to Jet when we get to the club and there won't even be an interview."

Lonnie did as he was told. And there wasn't an interview. After he opened the nuts, Jet gave Lonnie the grand tour. There was the ledger, the downstairs safe, and the upstairs books. Gave him a key to the desk. Even showed him the floor safe where he stored the cash for his father. But not the inside. Man was into bragging but the old man scared him. He also didn't say anything about the second safe next to it.

Lonnie asked, "What's in the other safe?"

Jet grinned, said, "I don't see any other safe." Lonnie put the floor panel back into place over the side by side safes. Smoothed the carpet over it. Said he didn't see any other safe either, must be the excitement of finally working for someone like Jet. Someone who was really going somewhere.

Jet was sold. Said, "I do have somewhere to go. You get stuck on anything or run into trouble, call me, okay?" Lonnie promised.

Jet and Carlos got into the Hummer. Wiggins said to Lonnie, "Let me know how it goes."

Lonnie shook his hand. "I got this." He watched them go. Looked at the muscle that stayed behind. "You guys have any problem with me?" They didn't. New boss same as the old boss, far as they were concerned. As long as he didn't step out of line. They had a drink on it. Then Lonnie called Big Maggie to tell her the news. He had a real job for the first time in his life and it felt good. Real good.

47

Gillian's was busy. Lights blazed and the pedestrians walking by were told, "Don't Stop Believing" from the open doorway. Inside, bodies were crushed together, many clad in legwarmers and parachute pants, and it looked like the whole city's supply of hair spray had been used.

Chuck sat at a table with Chris Sullivan. Venus brought three beers over, her jeans traded for dress slacks and a low cut blouse. Chris noticed while saying to Chuck, "You really arrested the wrong woman?"

"Everybody has done it."

Venus set down the beers, said, "Chris hasn't. Have you?"

"Nope." He gave her a big smile.

"Smooth," said Chuck. "You know she'll lead you on all night but never close the deal."

"What?" asked Chris.

Venus, "He's just trying to change the subject."

Chris said, "I think I'm missing something."

Chuck, obviously not on his first beer, said, "Let me spell it out for you, Kid. See, Venus here? You can be as sweet as you like and it won't matter. She may even drive you home, thank you, but you won't get as much as a good night kiss."

Venus patted Chuck's cheek, "There, there." She turned to Chris. "He's leaving a big part out of the story. This is just to distract you. I know you weren't hitting on me."

"I wasn't," said Chris.

"That's what I said," said Venus.

Chuck said, "Then stop staring at her boobs."

"Enough," said Venus. "Finish the story or I will." Chuck didn't like the way Venus told it, made him sound like an idiot.

"Fine." He took a drink. "We had the warrant and it was for this old lady and we went to the house but she wasn't there and her daughter said she was at the store 'cause it was the first of the month and she always shops on the first of the month and so we asked where she shopped and the daughter said." Chuck burped. "Excuse me."

He lost the thread of the story. Venus saw Mitch and Pete walk in, waved them over. Mitch said, "Glad you made it out, Kid. What are you drinking?"

"Don't know," said Chris. "Everybody keeps buying them for me."

Mitch said, "Venus, you want another? I see Chuck's out."

"I think Chuck's had enough," said Venus. "I'm going to run him over to Sharita's before he's useless to her."

"What?" said Chuck. "I'm not even feeling anything."

"That's kind of my point." She pulled Chuck to his feet.

Chuck leaned over to Chris. "Stop staring at them. She doesn't like that."

"Let's go, Chuckles." She dragged on his arm, turned back to Chris. "It's not that I don't like it, more like it's rude."

Mitch pushed through to the bar, Pete and Chris in tow. Gillian danced behind the bar with two other people, all mixing and pouring madly. She greeted Mitch who held up three fingers. As if by magic, three bottles appeared in front of him and she was gone.

Mitch turned to find Pete and Chris fully engaged, Chris saying, "And Chuck was all like, stop looking at her boobs."

"Sounds like Chuck," said Pete. "He gets like that, thinks he's the only guy allowed to look."

"But I wasn't looking."

"Sure thing, Kid." Pete took a beer from Mitch, thanked him. Mitch asked what he'd missed and Pete told him, "Your padawan was scoping out Venus."

"I was not."

"Oh, that's bad," said Mitch. "Only thing worse would be if you called her Angie."

"You didn't call her Angie, did you?" asked Pete.

"No," said Chris, very confused. "Why would I do that? Who is Angie?"

"She is. Venus." Pete looked at him. Looked at Mitch. Started laughing. "He doesn't even know her name."

Mitch said, "Pretty bad, checking out a girl you work with and you don't know who she is. Even if she is putting it right out there."

"I wasn't checking her out."

Pete said to Mitch, "You think he's not into that kind of thing?" Mitch shrugged, maybe.

"I'm into that." If there was one thing left Chris was sure of, that was it.

Pete said, "So you were checking her out."

Mitch drifted away. Pete would make that last all night and he saw Katherine talking to Cindy. Then he saw Ramon making for them too and picked up his pace.

Pete said, "If you ever want a full time spot on the warrant squad you've got to cut that out. Keep it professional at all times."

"Like you?" asked Chris.

Pete nodded. "Just like me."

Chris let that settle, then leaned in close and said, "So, one professional to another, what do you think my chances are?"

Ramon Restrepo had a similar question on his mind but he wasn't interested in Venus. He sidled up behind Cindy and put his arm around her. "Good to see you."

Cindy was startled, said, "Ramon." He suddenly recognized the woman she was with as Judge Katherine Silver. In jeans. Took his arm back from Cindy.

"Judge," said Ramon.

Katherine said, "Mr. Restrepo."

"I see neither of you has been served yet. Let me take care of that." He waved his arm, trying for a bartender. "This place is notorious for the terrible service." He kept waving his hand up and down.

"Practicing for later tonight?" asked Cindy.

"I would expect you to be a bit more polite in the present company," said Ramon.

"And I would expect you to be more not here."

Ramon snorted then pointedly turned his back to Cindy, focused his predatory smile on Katherine. He said, "We haven't gotten a chance to meet yet." He extended his hand. "I'm Ramon."

Katherine caught Cindy's warning stare. "We met in court, don't you remember?"

He did. "I meant personally."

"We've accomplished that now."

He turned the smile up a notch. It was almost scary. "I don't think I've ever seen a judge here before."

Cindy tapped his shoulder. "We're kind of in the middle of something."

Ramon said to Cindy, "And now we are in the middle of something," He turned back to Katherine, said, "May I buy you a drink? Would you prefer to move to a table? We could have a little more privacy."

"That is not what I would prefer," said Katherine. "As you know, one of the dangers for a judge going out for a drink with other members of the court family, including trial attorneys, is that personal relationships can develop and personal relationships lead to the appearance of impropriety, and you know where that leads, don't you?"

Ramon nodded. "Disqualification under 455."

"And when the relationship in question is between a judge and an attorney, the judge's duty to sit requires that the attorney be recused. I'd hate to put you in that expensive position. Mister Restrepo."

His smile shifted to a different sort of arrogance. "That's a bit presumptuous, don't you think? After a single drink welcoming you to the community that we'd develop a"- a drink spilled on Ramon. Sort of accidently poured all over him.

"Oh, man," said Mitch. "I'm really sorry, Ramon."

Ramon snapped his attention away from Katherine and zeroed in on Mitch. "You should not be allowed out in public."

"It was an accident. I must have bumped into the stool." Mitch earned a smile from both women.

"This shirt cost more than you make in a week," said Ramon.

"Just more of my unprofessional behavior, I guess."

Ramon moved, checked himself. Looked at Katherine. Said, "You won't always be untouchable, Kannenberg."

Mitch said, "But you will always be an ass."

Frustrated and embarrassed, Ramon slithered away. Mitch took his spot with the ladies. Asked Cindy, "You free on Saturday? I need a favor."

"Can't. My sister's kid has a thing."

He chuckled. "Really, though. Pete's having a party and the only way I could keep him from trying to set me up was to promise I'd bring my own date."

"I really am busy," said Cindy. "Sorry."

He waved it off. "What are you going to do, right?" He tried to think of something else to say, or talk about, but Katherine made him nervous. "See you around." Cindy nodded. He turned to Katherine, "Judge."

She nodded her head, "Marshal." Watched him walk away through the crowd.

When she turned back Cindy was looking at her. "What?"

"Nothing."

"Didn't realize you and Mitch had a thing."

Cindy laughed. "Not hardly. Mitch isn't with anyone."

"What was with the date?"

Cindy thought, said, "We've got an arrangement. Keeps things simple."

"Simple is good," said Katherine. Wondered fleetingly if maybe complicated might be okay too. It looked good in blue jeans walking away.

48

Lonnie made the last ledger entry at three in the morning. He was tired and his head hurt from the music and flashing lights. Slipping the extra cash had been easy but figuring out where to stash it proved harder. There was no way he was going to take it out of the club. He settled on the bookshelf in the upstairs office. From the dust it looked like Jet never touched it.

It was easier than he thought to get a cab back to Big Maggie's but harder to get inside without being noticed. She dozed on the couch and woke up when he came in. He was tired but she wanted to talk, see how his first night was. He owed her that.

His answers satisfied her. She promised to keep the others quiet in the morning so he could sleep. It wasn't the first time she'd surprised him, or that he was thankful that she'd scooped him up off the curb so long ago. He said as much.

"You're one of the good ones," she said, working on one step at a time up to her bedroom. "Too smart to stay on the street."

There was a time when that would have offended him, when he was proud of being second generation street. But not anymore. He thought about Charlene. Wondered if maybe she'd talk to him again, now that he was legit.

49

DeliMax was what you'd expect from a downtown sandwich shop, glass and chrome meat cases in a brightly lit room that was too small for all the tables and chip racks. A crew of five was busy with the lunch crowd and the line snaked out the door.

Mitch was a frequent customer, not because they were cheap or good, but because it was directly across the street from the courthouse. He waited patiently, got his ham and Swiss on white, and walked out.

Katherine sat at one of the outside tables, paperwork spread out and weighted down with a ketchup bottle. Her plate was off to the side and she didn't see him.

"Hello, Judge."

She looked up, felt a little funny. Said, "Hi. Almost didn't recognize you in your disguise."

He took off his shades, gave her the smile. She returned it. He said, "Better?"

She pursed her lips, "Turn a little to the left." He did. The sun shone on him, a slight breeze moved summer around them.

"How do you like it here?" asked Mitch. "Different from the big city?"

"Sure. I guess different is a good word, from what I've seen so far." She ate a fry. "I haven't actually gotten out much. Work is a bit more than I expected."

"So it's harder than just putting on the black bathrobe and saying overruled?" There was that smile again.

People pushed around him. She smiled back, said, "I also don't really know anybody."

"Sure you do," he said. His heart was pounding but he pushed in anyway. "One of them is standing right in front of you."

"So you are." She smiled back. "And you're blocking traffic. Why don't you go ahead and sit down since you're determined to interrupt the only peaceful moment I've had all day."

He took the chair, noted the way her hair was moving. She looked at him expectantly, half of the smile still lingering.

"So."

"You'll have to do better than that," she said.

He grinned. "Okay. Why did the fast rising big city attorney drop everything to become a stuffy old judge in a backwater town like this?"

"That's straight to the point," she said. He waited. "I'm a country girl, not a city girl. New York was exciting and challenging, but I didn't want to stay there. It was too impersonal."

He didn't buy it and she could see it on his face. She kept going, said, "I like the law, but what I love is justice. The City was all law, about money." She let some passion slip into her voice, a little disgruntlement. "Not right and wrong, it was about who shouted the loudest and found the best loophole."

Katherine lost her place in the story, wondered how it was she hadn't noticed his eyes before. She finished, "If I wanted justice, balance, I had to get out of there."

"You don't miss it?" he asked.

She laughed. "Hasn't been time. I haven't even unpacked my house."

Ramon Restrepo chose that moment to strut by, a dandy in another bespoke pinstripe. The sun was blinding in the reflection from his shoes and all he was missing was a walking stick. When he saw Katherine he veered over to the small fence that separated the tables from the rest of the sidewalk. "Good afternoon, Judge." He actually bowed a little.

Mitch watched him casually, a cat trying to decide whether or not to swat at the dog. Judge Silver said hello back.

Ramon said, "I couldn't help overhearing that you haven't had much of an opportunity to see our beautiful city. Perhaps I could interest you in a river cruise on Saturday? There are some amazing homes on the water, including mine."

"No thank you."

"Perhaps dinner?" he asked. "The Violet Club has a wonderful jazz quartet that's almost as good as their pasta." He looked at Mitch. "It can be hard for some people to get a table but I never have a problem." His charm was sticky but the confidence of the man was impressive. "I'll pick you up at six?"

Katherine was not ready for his come on. Not ready for the invite and certainly not ready for the assumption of a date. "I'm busy, sorry." She heard Cindy warning her not to accept a drink. "Actually, let me be a little clearer. I'm not interested."

Mitch chuckled. Ramon scowled at him then said to Katherine, "You can't just sit around if you want to settle in." He waved his arms around. "Get out. Mingle with some people." Another sharp glance at Mitch, "People with class."

Katherine's back went up. "I do get out, and I won't be just sitting around."

Ramon pushed on, "Wonderful. Where will you be? We might run into each other, perhaps have the drink that was interrupted the other night."

"Not likely," she said. "The marshal is taking me to a party."

Both Mitch and Ramon were surprised, but the fat lawyer reacted first, huffing out, "I'm sorry to hear that. I expected greater discernment from you." He took a few steps then turned back, "If you change your mind, or need rescuing, call me." He turned on his heel and was swallowed by the noon crush.

Katherine turned back to Mitch. He stared at her. "What?" she asked. "You serious?"

"Of course not," she said. "Why would I go to a party with you?"

"Because if that was serious, you'd have to give me your address so I could pick you up," said Mitch.

"Or you could give me directions so I could get there myself. Except I don't have a car yet so you would actually have to pick me up."

"And we'd have to set a time," said Mitch.

"A party is lots of people so it wouldn't be a date." Katherine looked at him. Liking the idea.

"And you'd have to call me Mitch," he said. "To keep it simple."

Katherine nodded. Their eyes met. "Simple is good." She offered him her fries. He took one.

50

Pete got the call on his cell phone. It was from Marshal Nueman, District of Montana. The chief was in his office too and they had him on speaker. They congratulated him, said to take his time tying up loose ends, they'd see him when he could get there. Did he have any questions? Pete said, "No." His questions weren't the sort bigwigs wanted to hear.

Pete looked around the squad room. Venus was on the phone trying to get somebody to drive by an address. Chuck was running database searches, teasing out an address for a bandit's girlfriend, a list of addresses and phone numbers crossed out beside him.

Pete hung up, got up. Said, "Be right back." Nobody even noticed. The hallway was a grand affair, exposed stonework, granite tiles, rows of doors with opaque glass and stenciled department names. It was cool and quiet and he was going to be leaving.

He realized his heart was pounding. Someone was walking at the end of the hallway, whistling, and he couldn't see who it was. He leaned against the stone. Closed his eyes.

"You okay?" asked Mitch in a very good mood, appearing as if by magic.

"Yeah."

"You sure?"

Pete stared at him vacantly, recognized his friend. "Yeah. Just ate something funny I guess."

Mitch went into the office. Pete heard the door shut. Felt it. That wasn't his office anymore.

He knew he should be excited. He and Patti had been talking about nothing else (except the baby) for weeks. It was a long shot and he hadn't gotten his hopes up. Now it was real. He knew he should tell them. The announcement would be out by email later in the afternoon and they should hear it from him first. But he couldn't face them.

Pete walked outside. The sun brought back a bit of normalcy. He called Patti, had to hold the phone away from his ear. Why wasn't he that excited?

He was tired of the hunt. A lake and fishing sounded good. The promotion sounded good. He was going to be a boss.

He was leaving the street. Like Steve had done. It made him feel old.

He went back inside. Stood outside the Warrant Squad's office door. He'd been through a thousand doors, gun out screaming his head off, wrestling people to the ground, deflecting knives, even shooting a presa canario. This was harder.

He put his hand on the knob. Turned it. Went inside. Told them.

51

Big Maggie opened her front door to let the Probation Officer come in. She was a slight woman in her late 20s with a dark complexion who dressed nice and had big brown eyes still bright with hope and the passion shared by true believers and the young. Maggie wasn't sure which of the two this girl was, but she thought she might like her.

"You must be Maggie," said the woman. "I'm Carmen." She flashed her ID then held out her hand. Maggie fought an attack of nerves, took a deep breath, and took it.

"What do you want to see first?" asked Big Maggie, shuffling down her central hall and hoping Carmen didn't see the dust. They toured the house, started in the kitchen looking for booze and then the bedrooms looking for drugs and weapons. The boys were very interested in the young woman but behaved themselves. That was one of the rules. And Maggie had given them a stern warning to stay back. Way back.

When they were finished, Big Maggie offered her a glass of iced tea and despite her own rule, Carmen accepted. They sat together on the front porch.

Carmen said, "So does he really have a job?"

Big Maggie said he did. "I don't know the address and I don't approve of the name, but it's a real job alright."

Carmen felt relief, let out her breath. She didn't realize she was concerned, or trusted Maggie, until she heard that assurance.

"I don't know why you do this, but I'm glad," said Carmen. "I have hope for Lonnie."

"Me too."

"If you think there's anything up, let me know?" She turned her big eyes on the old woman. "We can head it off before it's too late."

Big Maggie made a face. "Why'd you have to go say a thing like that?" She stood abruptly and went inside. At the door she turned back for a moment and said, "You can leave the glass on that table. I'll get it later." She vanished into the darkness wiping her eyes.

Carmen smiled. Maggie O'Donnell was the real deal. And she had hope too.

52

Jet posed at the end of a slightly presumptuous dock in baggy swim trunks and sunglasses. The wood was weathered but smooth, the water of Lake Dunn a deep blue that looked cold. Across the small bay he saw other docks and the houses that went with them. Deserted. Nobody came up midweek.

He stepped down onto the floating dock that held two jet skis. Sat on one and gripped the handlebars. He made engine and tire screeching noises. Then he slipped off and climbed back to the wooden dock. He tried to put his hands in his pockets but the trunks didn't have pockets. He was bored, no pockets made him annoyed.

Wiggins stood on the grass between the lake and the Rask cottage, a sprawling monstrosity of seven bedrooms and an industrial kitchen more accustomed to caterers than the frozen pizzas they'd all been eating. Jet walked up to him, noted that the man had pockets and was using them.

"Real nice up here," said Jet.

Wiggins knew his boss, had made it his business to know him better than anybody. "This place sucks."

Jet laughed. "We gotta go back to the city."

"Thought you said your father told you to lay low for a while."

"It's a big place." Jet started up to the house. Wiggins got out his phone and called Lonnie at Booty Island. Told him they were coming back into town.

Lonnie was cool with that. He woke up the kid sleeping in the DJ booth, a strung out punk went by Cho-Cho. Told him to find some of the other guys, get a party going. Cho-Cho didn't like that plan. His head hurt and wanted to puke.

Thing about Lonnie was that even going straight, he was still street and had spent plenty of time in lockup. He had that look and used it. Cho-Cho moved his ass.

When he was gone, Lonnie went upstairs and filled a trash bag with the extra cash he'd been keeping on the bookshelf. He brought up an ice bucket with a bottle of Jim Beam and clean glasses for the dry bar, just in case Jet was in his CEO mood. Finishing touch was a can of mixed nuts, lid off but freshness seal still intact.

Back downstairs, Lonnie made sure that nobody had adjusted the security cameras and he had a clear path from the back door to Big Maggie's Caprice. And a view of both safes in Jet's office. Satisfied, he took the bag of cash out back and put it in her trunk under an old quilt.

Cho-Cho got back with a half dozen hoodlums that did per Diem work for Jet. None of them seemed especially happy to be there but Lonnie had a way of convincing people to do what he wanted and when he put them to work an interesting thing happened to Booty Island. It looked clean and the floor stopped being sticky.

The crew complained about how much like real work it was. Lonnie said, "It's worth it. Jet's going to be happy with you."

They didn't think he'd notice. "He will notice there's a party though." They didn't see a party. "Go clean up, put on some decent clothes. Then get some girls. Make sure there's one for everybody and a few extra. Just in case."

He handed Cho-Cho some money. "Girls. You do anything else with this and you're done."

Cho-Cho said, "Yes, Boss."

53

The Hummer glided up to Booty Island before the night had even started but the place already looked alive.

Jet watched people heading inside, heard the music thumping. He looked at Wiggins. "What's going on?"

Wiggins said, "Looks like a party." They went inside.

The first thing Jet noticed was that there were an awfully lot of people there for it being so early. The next was there were a lot of girls. Then he noticed how well dressed his crew was.

Wiggins said, "You smell that?" Jet didn't. "It's disinfectant. Somebody's been cleaning."

Jet realized his feet didn't stick to the floor. A slow smile grew as he started bobbing his head to the beat. Some girls waved to him. He waved back. It was like being in a Motley Crue video.

Lonnie walked down the stairs, a dark green silk shirt with a white embroidered dragon hung untucked over his dress slacks. He paused dramatically, seemed to discover Jet by chance, and waved him in. Like it was his club.

Jet started toward him, annoyed suddenly. Lonnie met him half way. "Afternoon, Boss."

"What are you doing?" asked Jet, loud, over the music.

"It's a Friday night, party time." He caught Wiggins's warning. "I hope you don't mind. People wanted to get started so I went ahead and opened."

Jet looked around. Booty Island was popular. People wanted to party and they came to his club. His. Lonnie said, "You head on up to your office if you like. Let me know if you want to go over anything. I'll be down here."

Wiggins said, "That's a good idea, Boss." He led him up the stairs. Jet kept stopping to watch the dancing and drinking.

Once the office door was closed Jet said, "What's he doing to my club?"

"Managing it," said Wiggins. He noted the bourbon and nuts. "You want a drink?" He pointed. Jet saw them too. The smile came back. He dropped onto his brown leather couch, sprawled out.

"Yes, I would. And bring me some nuts." Jet suddenly liked the idea of having a manager for his club. A competent man who knew his place.

Wiggins poured the drinks and said, "I told you he was good."

Somebody knocked on the door. Wiggins opened it. Ginger was there. She looked good, maybe too much makeup, maybe not. Jet was more interested in the black stockings.

"You aren't supposed to be here," said Ginger. She floated passed Wiggins. He looked at Jet, man was paying him no mind. He walked out.

Jet stood. "You checking up on me now?"

"Somebody has to make sure you're being a good boy." She walked to the table with the bourbon. Poured herself a drink.

"I didn't say you could have a drink."

"What are you going to do about it?" Her look matched her tone, not the words.

He knocked the glass out of her hand, threw her against the couch. It was fast and she made a lot of noise.

Downstairs, Wiggins transferred the cash from Big Maggie's car to his own. He left some under the driver's seat for Lonnie. There was a lot of money for just a couple of days.

Back inside he pulled Lonnie aside. "You sure you doing the books right?

Lonnie said, "Your man without vision was taking a lot."

Wiggins thought about that. It changed things. Said, "New plan. You start making the man some money with this venture."

Lonnie said, "That's the easy part. What we need to do is get him to use the club to clean his other business instead of relying on his father."

"I'll look into that," said Wiggins. "You keep doing what you're doing."

Lonnie nodded. "I'd like to make some changes."

Wiggins told him to slow down. They both looked up when Ginger came downstairs, pulling at her skirt, smiling at them, still a little hungry. When she walked out Lonnie said, "Damn." Wiggins said to be careful.

54

Pete didn't stick around the Warrants Office. Everybody was working. They didn't want to talk about his move. He didn't want to talk about it either. Not yet. He hunted down the Chief.

Wasn't hard, Chief was in his office. "Just had an interesting call," said Pete, half through the doorway. Chief waved him in.

"Have anything to do with the email coming out this afternoon?" said Chief. Pete grinned. "Good. Congratulations. I'm sorry to see you go but it's a good move for you."

"Thank you." Pete looked around. Things were starting to feel different. "When do you think I should head out there?"

Chief leaned back in his chair. Looked at his wall of plaques and certificates. "That all depends."

Pete said, "I don't want to put you in a spot."

Chief laughed. "You don't do anything around here, you could leave tomorrow and it wouldn't make a difference." He looked over at Pete. "Not for what matters. Mitch will miss you but it won't impact courts or special assignments."

"So I should pack my bags?"

Chief shook his head. "Not until you're ready. It's a big move, from the street to the desk. Hard to go back."

Chief's phone rang. They waited for it to stop. Sat in the quiet for a minute. "Big thing," said the chief, "You want to make sure your bridges are in good repair."

Pete didn't know what he meant. "Make sure you're good with Mitch before you go." Chief's phone rang again and this time he answered it. Pete took his cue and left.

He ran across the street to DeliMax for a coffee and by the time he was back the email had come out. Twenty six promotions across the country. He was one of them. Pete Peterson, Supervisory Deputy United States Marshal, District of Montana, Billings.

The congratulations started pouring in on his Blackberry after that. Lots of teasing, more than a few asking if he'd lost his balls. He went back to his desk in Warrants.

Chuck was gone but Venus and Mitch were still there, planning a hit for Monday morning. He said, "Hey," and Venus said, "Now you're a super you don't bring coffee for anyone else?"

He apologized but she was kidding and gave him a hug. It made him feel different, like he was already outside. "I'm not a super yet."

Mitch asked, "When do you report?"

"Both chiefs said to take my time." He looked around. "I haven't talked to Patti about it yet."

"You should call your wife," said Venus.

"I told her I got it," said Pete. "Just we haven't talked about when yet. Probably have to sell the house."

"And find a new one," said Mitch. Pete hadn't gotten nearly that far yet. "Now we've got something to celebrate at your party."

"Maybe I should invite more people?" asked Pete.

"You should call your wife," said Venus. She had a sparkle in her eye, looked good. Alive. "You tell Patti that Mitch is bringing a date?"

55

Katherine ran into Mitch on her way out. She had her bicycle in the elevator and had changed out the pants suit she'd been wearing when he saw her at lunch.

"Nice bike," said Mitch.

She was embarrassed. More by her hair than the bike. "It gets the job done."

He nodded. "Gave up on the U-Haul?"

"Better gas mileage."

He remembered what she said at lunch. "You don't have a car yet."

She grinned at him. "No wonder the criminals shake in fear when they hear you're coming after them."

"I can give you a ride, if you like." Katherine wasn't sure. "I don't know where you live. It'd be like a dry run, practice for tomorrow. So I won't be late."

"You should be late. I won't be ready on time."

The elevator door opened. He blocked the door with his hand while she maneuvered the bike out. "See you tomorrow," she said.

He thought about asking if she wanted to get something to eat but changed his mind, said, "Tomorrow." It was for the best, he told himself. No reason to make things complicated.

Katherine pushed her bike out into the summer evening and thought about how hungry she was.

56

The Petersen's lived in a modest home on a cul-de-sac. It wasn't magazine cover material, but the backyard was surprisingly large and there was a summer cookout in full swing with a grill, loud music, and kids splashing around in the pool. Pete had set up a horseshoe pit and a volleyball net and now surveyed the scene in his favorite Hawaiian shirt, tan cargo shorts, and crocs. Patti slipped her arm around him, stunning in a sundress that told the world he'd married way up.

"You need to get out there and enjoy your party, Baby," she said. He kissed her.

"You know I love you." She kissed him back, laughing, and disappeared into the crowd of cops drinking beer with their friends and wives and dates while their kids tore the place apart.

Venus sipped a coke, laughed at Chuck who was well on the way to wasted. Sharita was on his arm, an ebony woman in her early thirties wearing a skirt that was too short, heels that were too tall, and jewelry that matched.

Chuck said, "All I'm saying is that he won't bring a date, not that he won't show at all."

"That's like a whole other bet," said Venus. "Of course he won't bring a date, Pete's baby could win that bet."

"What are you talking about?" said Chuck.

"How do you put up with this?" Venus asked Sharita. "I don't know how you ever catch anybody. Let me break this down for you."

Chuck drained his beer, burped, and tossed the can.

Venus shook her head. "The question is, does Mitch show up, drop off a twelve pack, and bail right away or does he stay to meet the hussy of the week?"

Sharita said, "Actually, Angela, I think the original way you asked him was how long would Mitch stay before bailing."

Venus looked at Chuck. He laughed. "Honey, you are the bomb." He smacked her behind. She squealed and jumped away, saw Mitch on the street with Katherine.

"Don't take the bet Chuckles, Mitch is full of surprises. I'll get you another beer." Sharita walked away.

They watched her. Venus said, "You got a good woman."

Chuck nodded, "She's special. I gotta wiz."

Mitch and Katherine walked up the path to the front door. They looked nervous together, his arm around a twelve pack of Fat Tire, hers on a bottle of Brooklyn Gin.

Their hands brushed as they reached the door, almost lingering. He looked at her and she looked back. The awkwardness replaced by an awakening.

"So how do you marshals do this?" asked Katherine.

"What do you mean?" He was off center, unsure of what had just happened. She was playing and he didn't know what it meant.

"Do you knock and announce or just kick the door down and go in?"

"That depends on a few things," said Mitch. "Factors. Mitigations." Staring at her.

"Mitigations?" she asked. "That's a new one on me. In the car you said to be careful, that Pete was dangerous."

"He is," said Mitch. "We should probably just rush in, not give him a chance to fight back."

"Is that what you do when it gets dangerous? I think I'd run away."

"You aren't running away now." He moved slightly closer.

"I'm not in danger." She looked up at him. "You're here."

Mitch felt his heart beating through his chest. She stared back at him with an intensity that terrified him. "I think we may both be in danger."

She licked her lips, almost whispered. "Do you want me to run away?" She leaned into him. "Or rush in?"

The door flew open, extinguishing the moment in its wake. Patti stood there, in shock.

Then everything exploded out. "Mitch? Oh my goodness. You came. I'm so happy to see you. How have you been? What did you bring? You didn't need to bring anything. You look great. Who is this?"

"Katherine, Patti. Pete's wife." He gave her a goofy look. "I hope you don't mind that I brought someone, Pete said it was okay."

"Mind? Are you loco? Of course I don't mind. Of course I also never thought you would bring someone! Has Mitch ever brought a woman to my home? I'm being rude. Hello Katherine, I'm Patti. Welcome." She stepped aside and motioned them in.

"Please, call me Kate. I don't know why Mitch insists on calling me Katherine."

Patti laughed, "That's easy. Nobody wants to kiss a Katherine. If you were Kate he might start to like you. Come in. Pete is going to shit." She followed them through the door shaking her head, Mitch brought a date.

Mitch slipped his arm around Patti, told her to stop causing trouble. They moved into the house, Katherine in tow. She was relieved to be away from the door, that moment with Mitch. But what if he'd kissed her? Right then and there?

Out back, Katherine got the feeling she was missing something. People were polite but there were too many secret exchanges, too many people had questions for Mitch that weren't being asked. It piqued her curiosity and she left Mitch to find Patti.

Patti was too busy flitting to talk but got her mixed in with a couple of the wives and a daiquiri. They didn't know her. No questions about New York. No questions about Mark. She relaxed. Had another daiquiri, let the sun hold her, and settled into the meandering drift of the afternoon.

She went inside to freshen up and spent a long moment staring at her reflection. "What are you doing?" The image in the glass seemed just as confused as she was.

She came back outside to find everyone watching an intensely serious three on three volleyball game. Kenny Loggins belted from the stereo. It was a hot summer afternoon and it was awesome.

Mitch defined cool, shades and a sports t-shirt over shorts. Steve and Pete backed him up, bulldogs on the verge of a heart attack, bellies pressed against t-shirts that used to fit.

On the other side of the net Chuck looked Olympian, shirtless and glistening with sweat. Chris Sullivan stood half a foot taller in direct contrast, his pale white skin blinding in the sunlight. They were fit, young and strong against the old men. Venus was their third, her brown hair pulled back in a ponytail, dark glasses and the intensity of a huntress.

Katherine found her way to where Patti stood holding the baby. Chuck missed a return and Sharita yelled, "What are you doing out there?"

Mitch served, his hand smacked hard against the ball. Ace. Patti yelled, "Do it again."

Another smack, this time Venus was there, returned it. The old men moved, talking. Bump, set, spike. Clockwork compared to the other team.

"They've done this before," said Katherine.

Patti said, "Steve was at the academy with Pete and Mitch. He was on the squad with them for years before he promoted out."

The old guys scored. Mitch served again and Chris returned it. Pete missed. Patti said, "Honey, you can't let him do that to you."

He blew her a kiss. Chris served, his eye on Venus instead of what he was doing. It went wide. Chuck said, "What was that?" Chris smirked, guilty.

Patti said, "Keep shaking it, Venus."

Venus said, "Focus, Sullivan. Keep your eye on the ball."

"Then stay in the back row," said Chris. Chuck told him to give it up.

Pete served. It was on again, skill and luck for a long volley. Katherine said "Why do they call her Venus?"

Patti said, "She came into the office, first day, all excited, you know?" Katherine nodded, half her attention on Mitch in the game. "Everybody's all like, hey, how are you? Who are you?"

Score. Cheering. Pete served again.

"And she said Marrs from A.P.D.," said Patti. "But Pete, my beloved, he crushes her, says," and Patti mimicked Pete, "Marrs from A.P.D.? That's ridiculous. Men are from Marrs."

Katherine finished with her, "And women are from Venus."

Patti laughed. "Exactly. She's been Venus ever since."

The old guys lost the serve. Venus scorched one in, Mitch was there, sent it back. She flew at it, bumping Sullivan, sending him staggering. Pete and Steve struggled but couldn't keep it in play.

Chris watched only Venus. "Girl on fire." She ignored him, went back to the line for another go.

Venus fired again and again Mitch was there, taut and ready, reading her, sending it back. Chris kept it going, Chuck moving, Sharita yelled, "Use your Kung Fu, Baby." Then Venus, airborne, saving it, spiking the point and rolling on the ground.

Chris helped her up, smacked her bottom as she walked by. She stopped.

"You did not just do that," said Chuck, stepping back.

Patti looked at Katherine. "Tell me he didn't just do that."

Venus said, "Did I give you permission to touch me?" She slid her finger across his cheek, gently, a caress.

He grinned, "No, Ma'am."

She slapped him. Hard. "Then don't."

The crowd erupted with catcalls and cries of "dog" and "owned." Chris tried not to rub his face, it hurt, but his grin never wavered. He turned to Chuck, said, "She wants me."

Chuck shook his head. "Don't ever say that again."

Venus served, hard and fast, right into the back of Chris's head. He dropped like a stone.

Katherine covered her mouth with her hand, shock warring with awe. Patti laughed hysterically, said, "I think I'm going to pee my pants."

The game moved on. Steve served like a desk jockey, Chris tipped it back over and suddenly the rhythm of the old guys was broken, Mitch from nowhere spiking hard, Chuck diving and missing, and the game over.

Sharita dove to the ground beside her man, parents quickly covering the eyes of their children. She yelled at him, said, "You call that effort? Get up and do it again. Right this time."

He laughed at her and she punched at him. He grabbed her hand, they began to wrestle and then everyone flooded the field. Steve's kids ran over and hugged their dad, cheering while he reached for his wife. Patti with Pete, bent over double from the exertion. He stood with a tired smile, took the baby as she kissed him, told him he was a sweaty mess.

There were families together, happy, celebrating their closeness. Chris watched it all. Saw Mitch and Venus alone. It became clear to him in an instant, two roads. The hunters and the caretakers. He took a step toward Venus.

57

David Rask was not spending the summer afternoon half naked playing volleyball. He stood at the rail of Raskal, his 75 foot Sunseeker. Uniformed crew catered for men in tailored dress slacks and their women.

The back drop was spectacular, manicured lawns stretching down to the river, deep piers with expensive boats moored alongside. Ginger crept up beside him, handed him a drink, and got a peck on the cheek for her troubles. She looked good beside him, had the jealous eye of men and women alike. She was like the Raskal itself, filling her guests with envious lust, forcing them to be content with just being there.

She said, "I'm going to lie down. Get out of the sun." Rask knew what she meant. He watched her go, thought maybe he'd follow in a little while.

Ramon Restrepo took the opportunity to approach.

"Lovely day," he said.

Rask nodded. "Not one to be spoiled by business."

Ramon bit his lip. "Some things shouldn't wait." He turned to look out over the water. Rask turned too, giving them a bit more privacy. "I've been hearing things."

"Like what?"

"Like Raj hasn't been home for a few days." Ramon was unusually delicate, almost tactful. It was hard for him, but he respected the elder Rask.

"I've heard that too," said David.

"I..." Ramon considered his words carefully. "Represent you in many areas."

"But?" prompted Rask.

"I think if he comes home with company you're going to need a firm recognized on a more," and again Ramon paused. It was hard for him to say. "A more national level."

Rask didn't say anything.

Nervously, Ramon added, "I'm not stepping away, I just, as your lawyer and friend, I think I would need help to make sure your interests were properly protected."

Rask looked out at one of the estates, a historic manor carefully preserved. He liked that house. Planned to buy it someday. One of the few yachts on the river nicer than his was moored at its pier. He had no intention of giving up on acquiring it.

He looked at Ramon. The man was pompous and abrasive but he was also smart and had taken good care of Rask over the years. He didn't ask the wrong questions and always cashed his checks without asking where the money came from.

"Do you have anyone in mind?" he asked.

Ramon let out his breath. "I've narrowed it down to a few, based on what I think might happen."

"Let's see what my partner does." Rask turned from the rail, they were done. "Don't call anyone until I tell you."

"Of course not."

His guests were being well cared for, content to graze and gaze among themselves. He went inside to find Ginger.

58

Jet was throwing his own party at the lake. They'd brought some girls back from the city and Wiggins had gone into town and rounded up everyone who looked bored. After that it was easy, anyone passing in a boat rafted up and joined in.

He felt like a king, glad-handing everyone and showing off with food and top shelf booze. He grinned like the Joker, popping in and out of conversations, kissing anybody he felt like.

He strolled onto the dock, enjoying the scenery. A couple of girls edged by him, laughing. He pushed them into the cool water. They shrieked and splashed him. He laughed, then jumped in beside them.

Wiggins watched from the house. Shook his head. The man had no taste, no vision. A young woman, half fox, slipped her arm around him. She wore a tight t-shirt over bikini bottoms and gave him the sort of look that makes a cold man warm inside. He spared a final glance for Jet then led her to the house. At least the lake didn't suck anymore.

59

Kurt Cunningham moved from the conference room table to a chart on the wall. Then to a file box. He tore through it until he found the scrap of paper he wanted. He darted back to the chart, compared it to a scrap pinned to a string that led to another scrap. Frowned.

There was no music. No pizza. No girls. Robert Something-or-other had left a few hours ago, refusing to spend another minute on the case. Kurt couldn't do that. He wanted Rask. He needed a break, a fresh lead.

But he couldn't break the code. He knew there was an answer in there somewhere, the books were too perfect. The call records too clean. Something in the mass of notes and records was the key.

The sun set outside and he didn't notice. He wouldn't have cared. The case was his mistress. Nothing else mattered.

60

The Petersen home emptied out gradually, the younger single crowd heading on to bigger and later things while the families rounded up tired children and searched frantically for missing shoes and swimsuits.

Patti got the baby to sleep and went into the kitchen. Venus and Katherine leaned against the island counter, picking at leftovers and complaining that they didn't need the food but couldn't stop eating it. Patti started on the dishwasher.

Venus said, "One time we went after this guy, never forget his name, Vincent Scarzazi, hadn't reported to his P.O. for a couple months. Chuck did this whole big workup, found where he worked but that he hadn't shown up, tracked down an ex-girlfriend who hadn't talked to him in forever. Finally Mitch said to just go to the house already. We knocked, nothing, so in we go – not locked."

Patti stopped to listen, Venus crammed a piece of broccoli into her mouth. There was green on her teeth when she said, "The smell was awful. Like dead body awful and I was pretty sure we were going to find a corpse but we didn't. The guy was on a couch surrounded by takeout containers and old chip bags sitting in a pile of what all that becomes. Told us he hadn't moved since the girl broke up with him. Said we couldn't make him leave."

She laughed, took a drink. "He was right. We couldn't budge him. Had to get the city to come in and they took out part of the wall."

"What happened to him?" asked Katherine.

Venus shrugged. "Don't know. I don't keep up with folks after we bring them in." Patti and Katherine looked at her expectantly, it felt like half of a story. "He ate a lot he didn't need to, couldn't move, and gained like 500 literal pounds."

Katherine said, "So?"

Venus frowned. "So we were just talking about eating when we weren't hungry."

Patti laughed and finished loading the dishwasher. Looked at the other two women. "Where's that bottle you brought us, Kate?"

She found the gin behind her toaster oven and set it on the island. Then she slid a chair over so she could fish three shot glasses out of the nether reaches of a cupboard mounted well above her reach.

Katherine said, "I'm not sure I'm up for shots."

Venus said, "Then we'll only do them one at a time."

Patti poured, taking the time to read the bottle. She and Venus each took a glass, raised them in a toast, and threw them back. They set the empties next to the third full one. Both of them waited for Katherine.

She shook her head. "This is unbelievable. I'm 38 years old and still giving in to peer pressure." Her hand darted out and seized the glass. She eyed it, as from the top of a high dive, then plunged in and tossed it back. The fire coated her throat and she couldn't help the shiver that ran through her whole body.

Venus smiled. Patti said, "You're 38?"

"Is that too old for you kids?" asked Katherine. Venus poured another round.

"It's not that," said Patti, raising her glass again. "To being older than we look."

Katherine glanced at Venus who shrugged. They both drank anyway before Venus said, "Don't you mean looking younger than we are?"

Patti considered it but wasn't sold. "What do you think, Judge?"

Mitch interrupted them, stumbling slightly through the sliding glass door from the deck. "Shots?" He chuckled. "This should be interesting."

He moved further into the kitchen, the scent of sweat and wood smoke trailing him. "Whatever you do, Kate, don't let Patti go swimming if she's had more than three of those."

He turned his back on the girls and pulled a six pack out of the fridge. Patti, arm on her hip, said, "Okay, so why do you bring that up now?"

He snagged a bag of chips then offered up his full attention. "Just worried about you." He leaned forward, gave her a friendly kiss.

"You're so sweet." Both hands on her hips now. She turned to Katherine, "Isn't he sweet?" Katherine nodded, smiling. Patti turned back to Mitch. "Mi hermanito del diablo. You better take the bag of pretzels for my Pete."

Mitch juggled the bag of pretzels into his arms, flashed the smile at Katherine. He paused at the door and said, "No swimming."

Patti threw a dishtowel at him, "Get out of here."

Katherine said, "What's with the swimming?"

Patti shook her head. "No, no, no. First I want to know why all of the sudden you're Kate."

"Katherine is an awfully lot to say." But she was wondering the same thing. Afraid that Patti had been right about why he only called her Katherine. Afraid that he was just being friendly and it didn't mean anything at all. She was being too quiet. "And he did have his hands full."

They stared at her for a minute. Then realized it was a joke. Patti nearly fell over, bumped into the island and then into a not quite empty 2 liter bottle of Coke which slid and sloshed to the edge and over. Fortunately it missed nearly everything except Kate.

Patti rushed over with paper towels. "I'm so sorry. Let me get that." She was a bit tipsy, uncoordinated, and her dabbing ineffective. When it started to get intimate, she stopped.

"It's okay," said Kate. "I'll be right back." She went to the bathroom, the door shut solidly behind her. They didn't hear her laughing.

"What is she doing here?" asked Venus, serious. "At your house. Drinking shots with us?"

"Mitch brought her.

"What's his rule?" Venus was agitated.

"Venus." Patti brushed her concern off with a wave of her hand.

"The one and only rule he never, ever breaks?" She wasn't going to be put off. It had been bothering her since he showed up and only gotten worse. She thought they'd even been holding hands through the fireworks.

Patti tried to settle her. "I think she's very nice."

Venus, "It isn't about nice. She works at the court house. He's always careful about that." Almost pleading. It was a rule she clung to.

"But they're just friends," said Patti. "She basically invited herself the way he tells it."

Venus shook her head. "You aren't that drunk. He called her Kate. He practically dared her to go swimming with you."

Patti smiled despite herself. That was not a story for tonight. "People change. You of anybody should know that."

Venus chewed on that, didn't like it at all. She muttered, "Mitch doesn't."

Patti hugged her. There was a hurt, somewhere. Uncertainty. But the closeness of the women was real and reassuring. Holding back, in the shadows, Kate wondered what she was getting into.

61

Pete and Mitch were all that remained of the manly men. Actually, there wasn't anybody else left at all outside with them. A small fire snapped inside of a perfectly arranged pit of patio paver stone. They sat in folding lawn chairs with their feet stretched out and bottles of Pete's own creation in their hands.

"I'm going to miss this stuff when you're gone," said Mitch.

"That beer's going to be gone long before I am," said Pete. He ate some pretzels. "Thanks for getting the chips, these are perfect."

"That's what partners are for." Mitch thought about Kate.

Pete watched him. "Your partner is of the opinion that you are considering the virtues of a very particular member of the female variety of our homosapienness."

"You've enjoyed your party a bit too much."

"Tell me about her," said Pete. "I can't believe you brought a judge to my house."

Mitch shrugged. "I told you all about it. We were at DeliMax and she told Ramon that I was bringing her here."

"Yeah, that doesn't cut it." Pete was sober enough to want more details.

Mitch laughed. "She doesn't have a car. That day we had court I ran into her on the street. She got into a U-Haul truck."

Pete said, "No shit."

Mitch laughed harder.

"Why is that funny?"

Mitch said, "I don't know." He settled down. Watched the fire again. "There's something about her. When we were at the bar all I could think was don't blow this. Don't be dumb."

"You were dumb."

"Was not." Mitch drank. "Maybe a little, but in a funny, charming sort of way."

"You tell her about Tara?"

Mitch turned a little too fast, almost fell out of his chair. "Geez, Pete. Why would I do that? We've had like four conversations."

"I just don't think you should wait too long." Pete, being a grown up. "You think this girl is special. You don't ever think anybody is special. You better treat her right. You don't want to drop that on her in six months. She'll bolt and you'll be alone."

"I'll have you," said Mitch.

Pete was quiet, finished his beer. "No. Not in six months."

Mitch finished his beer too. Popped two more open and handed one to Pete. "Buzz kill."

Pete said, "Sorry," and meant it. They watched the fire, listened to the snap of the dry wood and the crunch of the pretzels. "I just mean that you shouldn't hide it. She should know before you do anything."

Mitch looked at Pete. "Do anything?" Pete nodded. "What does that mean?"

"You know," said Pete. He waved his hands around, sloshed his beer. "Anything."

Mitch turned his chair to face Pete directly. Leaned forward. Said with the straightest face possible, which wasn't very at this point, "Do you mean like" – he stopped, looked over both shoulders, then whispered, "Sex?"

Pete said, "That's the most boring way to describe what's going to happen that I've ever heard. Dude, that's a Judge. Do you know that? Nobody goes there. Under the robe." He gestured and made a face.

Mitch laughed but it trailed off. "Nobody goes there because it's against the rules."

Pete now serious again too. "I didn't think of that." He looked around the yard, the remains of the party. "And everybody saw you here."

"We were good," said Mitch.

"You were holding hands," said Pete. Mitch couldn't help himself. He smiled. Content. It wasn't for long but it was real. Their hands just sort of found each other and they held on for a little while.

Pete said, "I have not seen that particular smile in a good long while." He stood. Teetered slightly. "I'm going to the bathroom."

Mitch stood. "Right now? Are you wearing Depends?"

"Funny," said Pete. "When I come out, you need to take your Judge home." Mitch clapped him on the back and they went inside.

62

Kate, she'd had way too much to drink to be Katherine to anyone anymore, let Mitch guide her out to the car. The night was clear with stars and a toe nail moon. She leaned heavily on him, took three or four times as many steps as she should have.

She thought Mitch was hilarious. Whatever it was he was saying. She couldn't quite figure it out. But it was funny. Otherwise she wouldn't be laughing. That thought was even funnier and she fell down, it was so funny.

He knelt beside her, strong and present. He looked concerned. And handsome. Holy crap handsome! She tried to kiss him but spit up a little instead. He helped her back to her feet. Then into the car.

He was very quiet in the car. She fell asleep. Mitch watched her, smiled every time she snored. He drove slowly. Partially not to disturb her. Partially because he didn't want the night to be over. It had to be the last time they were out like this.

He tried to wake her up when they got to her house but she was having none of it. He searched through her purse and dug out the keys. It was hard not to note the little things, lotion and chap-stick, gum, a tampon. Judge or not, she was a woman, just like any other woman he'd ever met.

Nothing like any woman he'd ever met. He carried her to the door. He set her on her feet so he could unlock it and she held on to him.

"Kate." She held on tighter. "I know you're awake."

She kissed at his neck. "Carry me inside."

He did, cursed himself for crossing the line even further. The boxes stacked in the empty rooms frowned at him. "I can't climb the stairs," she said.

He shook his head. She kissed him again and he let her. "Take me upstairs."

His protest never really formed even in his mind. He wanted nothing more than to take her upstairs. At the top he saw that one of the rooms had furniture. He carried her in and laid her out on the bed.

"Help me get undressed." She sounded more asleep than awake."

"You're fine." He sounded gruff. The words caught in his throat.

"Okay," she sat up, swung her legs over the side of the bed. "I'll help you get undressed." She reached out and fumbled with his clothes. He caught her hands.

"Kate." Nothing. "Kate, listen to me." Somehow she found his face, locked in on him. Smiled. "We can't do this. You're a judge."

"Objection over ruled." She laughed. Pulled her hands free.

"I'm serious. You know we can't do this again."

Kate held in her laugh. "Then it's tonight or never." She leaned back across the bed with her arms stretched out. "Your choice." Her vote was pretty clear.

Mitch fought, looked away. "Good night, Kate."

"Are you turning me down?"

"You're drunk." Mitch stepped back. "I don't want a one night stand with you."

She thought he was kidding. Laughed even. He carefully situated her on the bed. Pulled the sheet over her. Bent to kiss her forehead and realized if he did there was no going back. He caressed her cheek instead. "Sleep tight. Sorry about how you're going to feel in the morning."

She faded in and out and watched him through mostly closed eyes. Disappointment turning into wonder. Who was this man? She opened her eyes as wide as she could but he was gone.

He was back suddenly, with a glass of water and an open bottle of aspirin. He set them on her night stand. Noticed she was awake. He smiled at her. "You'll probably want those in a few hours."

She smiled back. Mouthed thank you. He blew her a kiss from a million miles away.

63

Patti held her man, on the verge of sleep. Content. More than that. Life was being kind. She kissed him and he stroked her hair. "I love you."

The baby started to fuss. They both tensed but he settled down. Life was being kind indeed. For the first time since he'd found out, Pete was truly at peace with the promotion.

64

Lonnie got back to the house just after 3 in the morning. It was routine now and he was quiet on his way in, didn't want to disturb anyone. There was a light shining from under one of the bedroom doors. That wasn't routine and he went in. Three of the boys were gathered around a computer screen watching something. He snuck over and looked.

It was a video feed from somebody's bedroom. He saw two people sleeping. They looked familiar. The couple from three houses down. "What are you doing?"

The boys jumped. The laptop screen was instantly folded shut. "Relax," he said. "How are you watching that?"

Clive said, "We did some yard work for them. When I went in to use the bathroom I put up a couple of cameras." The boys were nervous. "You gonna tell Big Maggie?"

"How hard is it?" asked Lonnie. "Put a camera like that somewhere?"

"Not very." Clive looked scared. "Big Maggie's gonna kick us out, isn't she?"

Lonnie shrugged. "Show me how it works. On the computer." They did. The live feed and then their favorite parts from earlier in the evening. Lonnie was impressed by what he saw.

"Tell you what, you help me out and I won't say a word."

65

Raj Rasheed leaned on the second floor railing and watched the cars out on the highway. There seemed to be a lot of minivans with car top carriers and stuffed animals pressed against the windows. He wondered where they were all going.

The door behind him opened and Connie stepped out of room 221. The Harcourt Motor Lodge wasn't the sort of place where she usually stayed but she wasn't complaining. She'd come from bed and wore a light jacket against the chill.

"Do you see him?" She put her arms around her husband.

"Everywhere I look." He turned, took her in his arms. "We can't do this."

"Do we have a choice?" Bitter.

Raj sighed. He had waited until after the wedding invitations went out to tell her about his association with David Rask, the special services he provided. It wasn't part of some grand design, he'd just been looking for the right time. It never came and each day brought more guilt. He knew he had to act, knew what the right thing was. She'd raged at him at first, told him he wasn't the man she thought he was. Eventually it came out that Connie was talking about keeping it a secret from her, not the criminal activity he was engaged in. She needed to be able to trust him.

He hadn't kept a secret from her since and after Jet left, when she was finished wrapping his wounds, she didn't question him when he said they had to leave.

She didn't question the random route, or the prohibition on calling anyone. And, other than a raised eyebrow the first night, she didn't question the motels they stayed at. She'd always known they might have to run.

She waited for him now, waited for him to reassure her. "There's always a choice."

She took his hands gently. "You need to see a doctor."

They heard shouting in the parking lot. "We should go in."

He thought about that as they closed the door on the world. He wasn't a fighter, not the way Jet was. And he'd run, there would be no reconciliation with David.

"I trust you," said Connie. He nodded. "You'll do what's right."

He nodded again. He didn't trust himself to speak. She turned off the light.

In the morning they loaded up the car, Connie drove because his hands were still too damaged. The girls sat in the back, lost in the fantasy world playing out on the little TV screens in front of them. They caught the red light for the interstate on ramps, North or South. After a moment's hesitation, she put on the turn signal. Going back. She looked at him. He nodded.

66

The conference room in the United States Attorney's office had been cleaned up. There were still boxes of files, but the table was clear and the maps and charts were gone. Kurt bounced around the room, Terry sat at the table, a laptop open in front of him. Across from him sat Raj, tailored suit and hands freshly bandaged at a hospital.

"Mr. Rasheed, these records are amazing," said Gaff.

"Mr. Rask likes exact figures."

Terry scanned spreadsheets and bank statements on the computer. "Is this everything?"

"Everything he had me handle," said Raj. "I don't know if there's more."

"And you're willing to testify in court?" asked Terry.

"Mr. Gaff, I am not a fool." Raj spoke softly, deliberately. "I knew before I came to you that I wouldn't get a deal for just the records."

Kurt pulled up a chair beside him. "You're okay with that?"

"Look at me." Raj lifted his hands. "What choice do I have?"

Raj took a sip of water. "Jet came into my home. To where my family lives. He beat me. Put his hands on my wife, threatened my daughters. My relationship with the Rasks is over whether I testify or not."

Kurt and Terry exchanged glances. This was a dream, an answered prayer, but it was too convenient. Kurt said as much.

"Would I do this to myself?" asked Raj. He hadn't expected them to doubt him.

"Would you?" asked Terry, "For your friend?" He held the other man's gaze for a moment. "Rask has taken some hits lately. Are you just being a team player?"

Raj sighed. "Do either of you have family?" Silence. "I didn't think so."

He sat back in his chair, closed his eyes. "When I was 7, first arrived in this country, my brother and I were walking down the street. It wasn't a nice street, like where you live. It was a dump, a slum."

"We saw Miss Lana pushing her stroller about half a block ahead of us. She was probably no more than 18 or 20. Four boys came out of an alley and started harassing her. Nobody on the street paid any attention. My brother and I watched as they poked at her, touched her places decent people wouldn't."

He opened his eyes, looked at them to make sure they were with him. "She looked for help but there was nobody but us and what could we do? The boys laughed at us too, they were big boys, older. They started pulling at her clothes, mocking her, showing off their power and cruelty."

Kurt sighed, impatient.

Raj eyed him coolly. "Then one of them tried to take her baby from the stroller. Do you know what she did, Special Agent Cunningham?"

Kurt shook his head.

"She became a wild thing. She shredded that boy with her fingernails. Her teeth. She pulled out his hair, gouged out one of his eyes, ripped his skin apart."

The scene was incongruous with his voice, the calm, patient cadence. "The other boys tried to pull her off but she fought them. Bloodied them all until they fled, pulling their friend with them. Even when she was too weak and terrified to save herself, she found the courage to protect her child. She thought of nothing but destroying the thing that was trying to take her baby."

On his face they could see the memory. He was still there, on that street. Kurt opened his mouth to speak but Gaff waved him to silence.

At last, Raj spoke again. "Fourteen years I kept books for David Rask but when Jet put his hands on my wife I knew I would have this meeting with you."

Raj's eyes glowed, passion seeped into his voice. "I'm terrified of the Rasks. I'm sure I will be killed for this." He settled again, certain of the truth. "But they will be punished."

Kurt was convinced. "I'll arrange for protection."

67

Mitch heard his cell phone ringing in the kitchen when he got back after his morning run. He found it in time, didn't recognize the number, and picked up.

"Thanks for the aspirin," said Kate.

He smiled. "How you feeling?"

"Pretty good, actually. I had fun." He had too. "You're a good friend."

He liked hearing her voice in the morning. And she didn't say friend like it was a bad thing. It wasn't an ending.

Kate said, "I'm going to lose my nerve if I don't say this now. I would really like to see you again. And please don't say something trite."

"I don't know anything trite."

"Like that." A pause. "I shouldn't have said it, I'm sorry. You were right last night. We can't do this."

Last night he was able to fight off temptation because she wasn't herself, not completely. He'd had that fear in the back of his head that it wasn't what she really wanted and if he'd done something she would never forgive him. Now she was saying what he wanted to hear and there was no doubt about what she wanted.

"Let a man speak."

"Okay."

"Okay." He said back. He grimaced. "I don't know if I was right about that. Maybe it's okay."

"It isn't," she said. "I looked it up. If anybody ever said anything you'd get in a lot of trouble. Maybe lose your job."

He didn't realize it was that bad. He wouldn't have taken her to the party. "I took you to a party of cops."

"And I had a really good time, as your friend."

"We held hands."

"Not for very long. Nobody noticed."

Mitch liked the way she was talking. "Somebody did."

She was quiet. "What if we don't hold hands anymore?"

He wanted to hold her hand right then and there. "This isn't a phone conversation. I can't think."

"Give me an hour," said Kate. She hung up. He looked at his phone. Saved the number. Stared at it. What was he doing?

68

It was almost 2 hours before the quiet of Kate's street was shattered by the rumble of his Harley. Mitch parked in her driveway, killed the engine and put his helmet on the handle bars. He squinted up at the flawless sky. Another summer day, baked with expectation and promise.

Kate stood at the door, a curious expression accenting her blue jeans and sweatshirt. "Mitch?"

He waved. Kate walked slowly over to the machine, her expression unchanging. He handed her the helmet that had been strapped to the back. "You'll want this."

She didn't move. "I don't ride."

He gave her the smile. It hadn't worn thin yet and she smiled back. "You don't or you haven't?"

It was a day for living dangerously. She took the helmet. "Where we going, Cowboy?"

"I'm going to show you everything." He climbed on. She swung up behind him, arms around him, tighter when he started it and the rumble moved through her whole body.

Kate was terrified at first. She fought him on every turn, convinced they were going over. "Move with me," he said. "Feel the motion."

She closed her eyes, let the wind and the engine sweep her away. The terror slid into fear and then wonder. The air was warm then cool, every smell instant and distinct and then gone. They swayed back and forth as Mitch drove through corners, following back roads flanked by rolling farms and woods.

They rode toward the mountains and thicker forest. She relaxed, but didn't loosen her grip. Their conversation was sparse and she didn't mind. There was no place else she'd rather be.

Mitch stopped at an empty pull-off beside a bridge. There was an old picnic table next to the state forestry sign and enough room for two or three cars.

He led her down a short path to the edge of the stream. It bubbled relentlessly, insisting that all the world be happy. The birds obeyed, the distinctive call of a jay was interrupted by the staccato beats of a woodpecker.

Kate ran to the edge and jumped across, hopping rocks to the other side. She looked over her shoulder. "Coming?"

They didn't walk far and in the isolation neither was shy about holding hands. "This feels right," she said.

"But it isn't."

"We could make this work. If we were careful." She took a step. He didn't follow. "Weekends here and there."

Mitch shook his head. "I wouldn't be able to look at you during the week. I don't think I could stand it."

She laughed but saw he was serious. Maybe she was too. "Besides," he said, "Somebody would find out."

"Not if we were careful."

"I've been hunting fugitives for 20 years. Somebody would find out."

"So why did you bring me out here?"

Now it was his turn to walk away. He picked up a rock, small and smooth. He spun it out over the stream and it skipped to the other side.

"Why did you come?"

She picked up a rock, heavy, needed both hands. He heard her walking up behind him. Couldn't face her. The rock landed in the water at his feet, splashing them both.

She laughed at him and he pulled her into an embrace. He said, "We could be careful, right?"

69

Jet lay on the couch in the main room of the lake house. He was in his underwear and a puddle of drool soaked the cushion. There were bodies all around him, stinking of sweat and vomit. The air was heavy with stale smoke. Nobody moved.

David Rask made his way through them. Stopped at the couch. He shook his head. Jet could have been so much more. He blamed it on video games and movies. That was easier than taking responsibility himself. He kicked the couch.

Jet said, "Beat it." Still asleep, very hung over.

David yanked him to the floor. "Get up."

"What the?" Jet struggled to focus, to get up. He was angry enough to almost make it. Then he saw David. "Dad?"

"Make me some coffee. We need to talk." David stalked to the kitchen. Jet followed, stumbling, hand on his head, hair spiked out everywhere. He looked awful.

Jet found the coffee pot but hit a road block after that. How the hell did you make coffee? "I'll get Wiggins."

David stopped him. "Forget it. I don't want coffee anyway."

Jet, irritable, "What do you want then?"

"I want to know why you've been back in town after I told you to stay away."

"I haven't."

David glowered at his son. "Is that your final answer?"

Jet wanted it to be, but he caved. "I only went back a couple of times. To check on the club."

"I let you get away with a lot of things but in return I expect you to do what I tell you." He looked through the refrigerator. "I expect that when there's something important that has to be done, something that impacts all of us, that you'll do it."

"I'm sorry." He meant it. It didn't matter.

David said, "I hear about your truck being in town again and I'll send you to Alaska." He walked out.

Jet watched him go, a hundred things he wanted to say and all of them trapped behind a headache this big. He slumped on the table. His foot kicked something. He looked, saw one of the girls from the party curled up in a pile of puke.

Jet went back to the couch.

70

Gibby's Diner transitioned flawlessly between the Sunday morning breakfast crowd and the Sunday after church lunch crowd. Pancakes gave way to lamb chops, hangovers to neckties and bonnets. Nobody paid too much, or expected too much, and everyone was happy.

Mitch's Harley leaned comfortably in the parking lot, helmets on handlebars and the soft tick of its cooling engine. Inside they sat across from each other in deep, animated conversation. They didn't notice the food on their plates. They didn't notice anyone else around them in the crowded restaurant. They didn't think about the future and the rules that promised heart ache.

Kate had forgotten joy. Getting the judgeship had felt more like escape than achievement. Mitch made her feel like she was the only woman in the world. As far as he was concerned, she was. Looking at them was to drink from the fountain of youth, to have hope restored.

71

Booty Island was deserted. And like the legendary place it was named for, Lonnie knew there was hidden treasure just waiting for somebody smart enough to find it. He escorted Clive through the club, showed him around, all the while feeding him a story about increasing security and concern that the employees were skimming.

Clive didn't really care, wasn't sure why Lonnie cared, but was in such fear of being kicked out of Big Maggie's house that he listened politely and installed a network of wireless surveillance cameras as instructed. He put them around the outside, in the entry way, the DJ booth, behind the bar, around the club floor, in the stairwell, and at angles that covered the entire upstairs office.

Lonnie stopped him when he wanted to put them in the rest rooms. Clive said, "A lot goes down in a club's bathrooms. You said you wanted to be able to see everything." Lonnie thought about a guy he bunked with in County who told him about finding jewelry in a toilet bowl tank. He said okay, cover it all.

Clive set him up with a laptop too. Seemed that Lonnie had plenty of cash for the project. It was an investment. Thing about technology was if you understood it, you had the advantage. The knuckle draggers that Jet hired didn't get tech. Not really. They knew what was on the street but not how it worked. Jet's security system was pretty good, but he didn't know how to use it. And now Lonnie's was better.

When Clive left, Lonnie called Wiggins.

"It's a new week."

Wiggins didn't really care. Lonnie asked, "You guys going to collect?"

"Why do you care?"

"I was thinking we could wash some of it through the club instead of passing everything to the old man."

"What do you know about money laundering?" asked Wiggins.

"Enough."

Wiggins wasn't sure. Wanted to be convinced. "How would you do it?" Couldn't keep the greed out of his voice.

Lonnie smiled. "Less you know the better, right?" Wiggins told him to sit tight.

72

The Harley growled up a mountain road, threading between the trees, with occasional cliffs rising and falling to either side. Kate was comfortable, leaned with the bike, held Mitch with less terror and more affection.

He pulled off onto a dirt track that opened into a small rutted clearing and killed the engine. The view was spectacular. It was as if the entire world dropped away from them. Fields and rivers stretched as far as they could see.

Kate climbed off the back and removed her helmet. She stared at the view. Shook out her hair. The sun was hot now that they were stopped and she peeled off her sweatshirt, tied it around her waist. She had on a Van Halen t-shirt and Mitch grinned.

She walked over to the edge and looked out. Mitch watched her from astride the bike.

"What is this place?" she asked.

He worked his helmet strap. "It's the place where you can see everything."

She smiled for him. "It's amazing."

"I like to come up here when things start to get complicated." He climbed off the bike and watched as she walked around, the sun on her bare arms.

"How far can you see?"

He thought for a moment. "Three or four states, on a clear day."

She looked at him. "What about today?"

"Today?" He moved toward her. "You can see the city, easy. Probably a lot farther."

"What about you?" Her smile changed a little, she leaned against a pine tree, felt it sway in the breeze.

"I can't see any farther than you." He was there. Close. His hand on the trunk of the tree over her head. His eyes drawing hers in.

She looked away. Muttered something

"Up here everything drops away. All the worry and fear and doubt. You're above it, you know?" He spoke quietly, sharing a secret he didn't even realize he knew. "Things fall into place. The world. Life." He looked out. "You see all that and everything else seems simple."

She looked at him then looked away again. Her breath kept catching in her throat. "There's nothing simple about this."

He kissed her. Gently, deliberately. "It's very simple."

She forced herself to meet his gaze. Felt the draw, the simplicity. He was right. She pulled him in and the kiss was longer, passionate. A release.

The sound of tires on gravel reached them through the emotion. She pushed him away abruptly, the fear of discovery, of what was happening, sharp on her tongue.

Mitch stared at her, stunned and hurt, confused. Annoyance at the interruption clouded his features as she slipped from the tree.

A Porsche roadster pulled up beside the bike. An older man climbed out of the driver's side, not looking at them. The young woman with him was drunk and gawked at them, an open bottle of wine in her hand.

The woman put her finger to her lips clumsily, poked her nose, laughing. "A secret." She shushed loudly. "Don't worry, I won't tell." She looked around. "We're not supposed to be here either."

It wasn't classy. Or special. It made Kate feel dirty. The man laughed and pulled a picnic basket from the car. They moved into the trees and out of sight.

But they were loud. Still intruded.

Kate walked back to the bike. Unsteady. She struggled with the straps of her helmet. Mitch followed, tried to help her. She growled at him. "This is stupid. Why can't I get it right?"

Mitch wondered the same thing.

73

Kurt spent his Sunday at the office. He called Terry so many times that the lawyer shut off his phone. "I'll be there in the morning. Don't call me again." Kurt had waited almost an hour before he called back, left a string of detailed voice mails, and went back to his computer.

The Rask case was big. He'd identified nearly thirty associates and pieced together the shape of the operation. The only thing he'd been missing was the proof. Now thanks to Raj he had it and it was time to roll everything up.

He typed out warrant applications. He rebuilt the case presentation. He assembled arrest packets and assigned team leaders. It was nearly dark when he finally finished. It was an Opus and he was happy.

Kurt double checked everything then called the SAC, James Reginald Burton the third, to get on the schedule for Monday. He wanted to move, wanted to get everybody involved, arrest some bodies, and prosecute Rask.

Call went to voice mail. He wrote an email, clicked the red exclamation point and hit send. Five seconds later he received an out-of-office. Two weeks till Burton would be back.

Kurt called the ASAC, Mathias Greene. Mathias said, "Don't call me on the weekend unless you are dead. Call my assistant in the morning and set up an appointment."

"This is urgent. I should have the warrants tomorrow afternoon and want to do the sweep tomorrow night."

"We're not doing anything until James is back," said Mathias.

"This can't wait two weeks," said Kurt. "I've got a protected witness." He was wasting his breath, Mathias had already hung up.

Kurt tried Terry again. Maybe if he could get the U.S. Attorney to push. He said as much in the voice mail.

74

It was a long ride back to Kate's house. She still held on, but not very tightly. There was a cool distance between them now. Didn't matter that he knew there had to be. All he could see was the sudden horror on her face when they were discovered, instead of her arms holding on he felt her hands pushing him away.

She had kissed him back but there was no hope in that anymore. He practiced what he'd say, when they got to her house. Tried to find the right tone and words but it was hard, he barely understood how he felt. How could he share that with her?

When they finally arrived he didn't say anything at all. She gave him back the helmet, said thank you as polite as could be, and practically ran inside. He wanted to just pull away but couldn't take his eyes off of her. Or the door long after she'd closed it.

At length he did go, the Harley roaring its own displeasure. Kate turned from her window and sank to the floor, her back against the wall. She felt like crying and that made everything worse.

He was just a marshal. Rough around the edges, arrogant, violent. Handsome and tender. Her fingers brushed against her lips. If he'd come to the door her resolve would have caved. She felt his warmth against her. Saw the hurt in his eyes.

Kate never expected him to give up so quickly.

75

Venus stopped by the Ops office on her way in on Monday morning. Steve flagged her down. "New DEA warrant for you guys."

"Anybody we know?"

Steve shook his head. "Nobody I recognized. Probably isn't even in the country."

She took the paperwork. When she got to Warrants, Mitch was already there, on the phone with someone about a lead they'd sent out last week.

Pete and Chuck came in behind her, laughing. They kept talking while settling in. Mitch told them to shut up, he couldn't hear.

Pete said to Venus, "What's his problem?"

When he was off the phone she told him about the new warrant. "What do you want to do?"

"Give it to Pete. He's got the hook."

Pete shook his head. "I've got to close out the cases I've already got, I can't take a new one."

"Why not?" asked Mitch.

"I'm transferring, remember?"

Mitch had forgotten. The full weight of Pete leaving smashed into him, a fifty car freight train that didn't even slow down.

Pete broke the awkward silence that followed. "Have to admit, I figured if you did actually bring somebody to the party it would have been Cindy, not a judge."

Venus said, "Yeah, what was that all about?"

Mitch said, "Nothing."

"Nothing doesn't hold hands," said Pete.

Mitch shook his head. "Sometimes it does."

"Sorry," said Pete.

Mitch said, "Chuck, why don't you take the case."

Pete's cell rang. They listened as a lead came in. "Must be good," said Chuck. "He's writing it down."

It was good and they rolled out.

76

The city didn't break down all at once. Different sections failed in different ways, sometimes to be reborn and sometimes not. The house that Pete led them to was in an area that had started to be reborn about two decades before. A backhoe rusted at the edge of a foundation line, stagnant like the promise it had brought.

Chuck took the back, dodging around cars and boxes of old clothes. The windows were caked with grease, kibble pushed hard against the fogged panes. The siding was probably ochre when it went up, now it was mud splattered, sap stained, and cracked in a million places. A fire escape had been tacked on the side of the house and it was as rusted as everything else.

The front stoop was cinderblocks, held together by sweat and gravity. The blocks were crumbling and stained with ash. Beer cans and butts paved the walk and covered the dirt yard. The marshals saw it all, but paid no more attention than a cheetah to the savannah grass.

Pete pounded on the door. There was movement inside. "POLICE! Open up."

More movement. Muffled voices. Venus stepped off the stoop and took up on a corner, pistol in hand.

Pete pounded again. "U.S. Marshals. Open the door."

"No." The voice was muffled, sounded female.

"Bridgette, I'm coming through the door," said Pete. "You can open it or replace it."

"He's not here," said the voice, presumably Bridgette. "He left this morning, before I got up. I don't know where he is. Go away."

Pete looked back at Mitch. "Just once, you know?" He shook his head. "Just once I'd like to hear something original."

They heard scraping from inside. Pete frowned. "She's blocking the door," said Mitch. They kicked together.

The door splintered open revealing a house as filthy and crowded as the yard had promised. A young woman in her early twenties struggled to move a table against the door. She looked strung out, hair a wild mess and bones stretching her skin. She stopped short when the marshals came in.

"He's not here," said Bridgette. Pete motioned for her to turn around. She motioned for him to screw himself. Venus came through the door, all business, backed up Mitch in the search.

He tore the place apart. Pulled doors off hinges, dumped drawers and overturned furniture. Venus tried to settle him down. "Place is a dump," he said. "Nobody could tell the difference between before and after."

Bridgette had a fit. Pete tried to calm her down but she wasn't interested. They found a healthy cache of marijuana but not her man. She spit at them on the way out.

Mitch turned on her, grabbed a handful of hair and dragged her onto the lawn. She fought, kicking and scratching, but was no match for him. The cuffs went on hard. She screamed in pain. He yanked her up and she screamed again.

Pete said, "Easy." He tried to take her. Mitch told him to open the car. There was a stare down, Bridgette whimpering in the background. Venus opened the door, took the girl from Mitch. "What's the matter with you?"

"That was assault, you saw it," said Mitch.

"Yeah, it was." Pete agreed. "What were you thinking?"

"I'm talking about her, Jackass."

"What does she weigh? 80 pounds with the crack pipe?" Pete shook his head. "You were not being assaulted."

Mitch glared, on the wrong side of the edge. Pete said, "Take a walk. I'll wait."

"Sure you won't be in Montana?" Mitch knew he was acting like a jerk but couldn't stop. Everything had been fine. Now nothing was. He took the walk.

Venus went over to Pete. "We're going to take her down to St. Mary's." Pete raised an eyebrow. "He broke her wrist."

"What's going on with him?" asked Pete.

Venus took a turn raising eyebrows. "Things aren't exactly going his way."

77

Venus caught Mitch in the parking lot of the courthouse on her way back from the hospital. "You talk to the chief?" she asked.

He shook his head, "Why?"

"Because you trashed her house and broke her wrist."

Mitch laughed. Venus didn't. "You're serious?"

"It would be better coming from you." She looked away. Heard him laugh again, cold and bitter. "You're the best man I know. This is not a road you should travel."

"Pete's probably already said something."

Venus looked back at him. "Pete isn't the problem. You can't expect him to stand in your shadow and do this forever."

"You leaving too?"

"Give me a reason to stay." It sounded more like a movie line than she intended. "Show me you haven't checked out."

"I haven't." He sounded a little bit like himself.

"Talk to the chief," said Venus. "And then go talk to the girl who's obviously not nothing."

"Why bother?"

"Because I've never seen you quit before."

78

Kate didn't feel like looking at another case citation. She felt like riding a motorcycle. But she had to look at the cases and couldn't ride the bike so she bucked up and carried on.

Cindy cleared her throat from the doorway. "Mitch is here, wants to talk to you about a search warrant."

Kate frowned. "Search warrant?" Cindy shrugged. "Send him in."

The first thing Kate noticed was that he looked awful. The second was that she didn't care. Then pro and con lists started forming in her mind about him being in her chambers.

"Why are you here?"

"I don't like how we left things, Kate."

"Don't address me as Kate when you are in my chambers." She put some sauce on it.

"I was hurt when you pushed me away up there, on the hill." He looked out the window. "I thought you felt something."

"I don't remember you asking me how I felt."

"You kissed me too."

She was business. "What do you want?"

"I don't want this." He waved his hand aimlessly. "I'm miserable."

"Why is that my problem? You drove away without a word."

"I'm sorry." He looked it. "I shouldn't have done that. I didn't want to do that."

"I didn't want you to."

Hope flickered in his eye. "So let's get back to it."

"Back to what? A secret tryst that breaks every ethics rule on the books?"

He was confused. Kate said, "Last weekend was our chance. Nobody could fault us for a friendly outing exploding into something more because on

Monday we could have walked in here and said whoa, that was a mistake and it won't happen again."

Mitch wanted to stop her, tried to speak, couldn't find the words or a break.

"We can't try to fix this because we aren't supposed to have it in the first place." She wasn't angry and it didn't sound like hurt. Disappointment was a better fit. "We had one chance and you drove away."

Mitch offered, "We could meet out of town."

She stood. "Marshal, you told me that couldn't work."

He stood. He remembered the conversation. She walked him to the door. "I'm sorry. I can't overrule this one."

He walked out. She shut the door and went to the window. Outside it was summer. She shivered.

Ramon sat in the reception area of Judge Silver's chambers making small talk with Cindy when Mitch came out. The small man was surprised to see Mitch and said as much.

Mitch looked at him without recognition, then with a sort of hatred. "What are you doing here?" he said.

Ramon smiled his courtroom smile. "I have a motion before Judge Silver. What are you doing here?"

Mitch couldn't think. Couldn't actually see very well. It was a bad moment in a bad day. "Search warrant."

Ramon smirked. "Looks like you came up empty handed."

79

Mitch did a lot of cleaning that night. Even found his mop. He scrubbed, scoured, and vacuumed until he was too tired to stand. It didn't help.

The chief wasn't thrilled about what had happened earlier. Was even less thrilled when he found out that Bridgette had actually broken her wrist and that the service was going to have to pay for it. He didn't threaten because he didn't have to. He also didn't say he was referring the matter to Internal Affairs for the same reason. The way his day was going, Mitch thought it was pretty likely that the Office of the Inspector General out at Main Justice would keep his case, or even Civil Rights.

Mitch started rearranging furniture, but he stopped because it made his house look like Kate's, all jumbled and disordered. He took a beer to his back porch and watched full dark settle. Shifted his mood from self-pity to guilt. He wondered if the rules would let him be with Kate if he lost his job.

He couldn't shake the hurt of being pushed away and laughed at himself. Big tough guy reduced to a moody child because a girl didn't want him. Had it really been that long since he'd cared about anyone else?

He didn't wait around for the answer. He moved on to another beer and felt rain. A few drops at first and then a deluge. Perfect. He raised the bottle in a salute that was only a little sarcastic.

80

Jet brooded. They were all stuck inside and it reminded him that he wasn't doing anything fun. He'd grown tired of playing quick-draw in the mirror. Grown tired of TV. Grown tired of the sidelines.

Trey pushed up from the couch on the other side of the room where Sleepless in Seattle played on the big screen. "I'm done." He walked toward the door.

"Where you going?" asked Jet.

Trey turned. "Out of here. This is a waste."

"We're not going anywhere," said Jet. "The old man wants us low."

Trey said, "He wants you low. Not me." He walked toward the door.

"Sit back down."

Trey stopped. He even turned. But he didn't sit. "No. I'm tired of your shit. Do this, do that, don't do whatever. Enough already."

Jet stood. "You work for me. I'm the boss. You sit down when I say sit down."

"I quit," said Trey. He looked at the faces now turned from the television to him. "That means you aren't my boss and I can leave when I'm done."

"You aren't done until I say you're done." Jet had white powder under his nose. Trey hadn't seen that before, might have made a difference before, but it was too late now.

Wiggins said, "Trey, why don't you come back over here. I'll get you a beer."

"Shut up," said Jet. "He wants to be done?"

Trey didn't like the edge. "I meant with the movie. I just need a little air."

Wiggins stood up. "Jet, let me take him for a walk. It's cool."

Somebody muted the TV. Paused it, actually. Rain slammed against the windows, pounded on the roof. Trey fidgeted. Wiggins said, "Jet?"

Jet mouthed something. They heard the muttering but couldn't make out what he said.

"Tell you what, how about I just sit down? Like you said." Trey stepped toward the couch.

Jet shook his head. "No. You want to be done. You want some air. You quit." He laughed a little. "Nobody quits. I got no place for quitters here." He laughed again. "Or people who don't work for me."

Jet looked at the couch of men. "Doesn't make sense to keep somebody around who isn't part of the team, right?"

Wiggins said, "Easy, Boss."

"It is easy," said Jet. The 45 was really loud and by the fifth shot they were all deaf. When the magazine was finished Trey stared lifelessly at the vaulted ceiling. "Now you're done. Now you got plenty of air."

Jet laughed, a little crazy, swapped magazines. He looked at the men again. They turned back to the TV. Wiggins said, "I'll get that cleaned up."

Jet shook his head, "Somebody else can do that. I want you to take me to my father's house."

81

Carmen was the rare public servant who loved her job. Not just the first day or week, but even now, six years in. She'd had some heartbreaks in the beginning, before she understood that a probation officer couldn't save someone who didn't want to be saved, but she'd seen a few turn the corner and that made it all worthwhile.

She double checked her hair in the rearview, retouched her lipstick. Practiced a smile, then scowled. It wasn't a date. She hopped out of her Rav 4 and started across the hot parking lot.

She hoped that Lonnie had turned, but also knew that hope was a dangerous thing. The job he claimed to have seemed too good to be true and when she'd first pulled in to Booty Island she was pretty sure it was, but there she went anyway.

Lonnie met her at the door and brought her inside the club. It was cool after the summer sun and surprisingly clean. He gave her the nickel tour and she started to change her mind. It was a ghetto club, but one of the nicest she'd ever been in. He poured her a diet coke at the bar and sat on a stool next to her with an ice tea.

"You really working here on the books?" she asked.

He smiled at her. "Everything's on the up and up, I keep telling you." He did keep telling her and she kept wanting to believe him. "I showed you the tax form, right?"

Carmen liked that he didn't get upset when she asked him over and over. "You did. And your pay stub."

"Not sure what else I can show you. I'm the manager so the only boss you could talk to is the owner and I don't know where he's gotten off too."

Carmen knew that too. It was actually what concerned her most about the whole deal. Jet Rask was notorious. She secretly hoped that the reason he'd disappeared was that he was dead. It went against her usual nature but some people were just scary evil.

Lonnie opened a can of mixed nuts and passed them over to her. "Fresh can. No grubby paws been in there."

She smiled at him and, despite her rules, took some. They were salty. She took another handful. "I'm really proud of you, Lonnie." She kicked herself. It sounded condescending.

But he lit up. "Really?"

"Yes." She snuck a cashew. They were good. "You seem surprised."

"Nobody's ever proud of me." He sounded sincere and had just the right touch of emotion, not breaking down and getting mushy, but not fake. "Thank you. That really means something, coming from a P.O." He looked at her. "Coming from you."

She felt a flash of heat. "Don't get the wrong idea."

He chuckled. "Girl, I ain't going there." He sipped the tea. "Not saying I wouldn't, don't get offended, just that I know what we have is a business relationship."

She nodded. "You'd be surprised how many people don't get that."

He waved his arm. "Brother's got one thing on his mind when he gets out."

"Not you?" Carmen was genuinely curious.

That chuckle again, with a real smile. "I came out with two things on my mind and staying out was number one." He looked around. "Didn't expect this."

Carmen noticed that her hand didn't stick to the bar. "Me neither."

"You know Big Maggie don't like a lot people." He was standing. "But she liked you. Told me I better not mess this up."

Carmen stood, got her purse. "What do I owe you for the coke?"

"On the house," said Lonnie.

Carmen shook her head. "I can't accept that."

"Soft drinks are on the house for everybody." He pointed at the shelf behind the bar. "You only pay for the hard stuff. And to get in when we're open."

They walked to the door. Carmen said, "Stay clean."

There was a moment. He nodded. "I will."

She walked back into the blinding sun. Lonnie stayed in the shadow of the door. "I mean it. And if you can't, let me know straight up. I can't help you if you play games."

"I won't play games with you." He said it like he meant it. The same way he'd said he would go there, in different circumstances.

She felt his eyes on her while she walked to the car. Considering. It was a good deal for him. He seemed sincere. She gave it an extra shake.

Carmen drove away thinking it was definitely too neat, too perfect, too good to be true. But she was giddy and hoped just maybe it wasn't.

82

Mitch sprinted across the parking lot behind Venus, BagDog 20 yards ahead of them. He was flat out and the two of them were pulling away. He called for her to stop but she either didn't hear him or ignored him.

The traffic stop hadn't gone quite as planned. They boxed the juiced up Honda okay but when Chuck and Mitch went to pull out the fugitive he'd hit nitrous or something and the car skidded sideways pinning Chuck against the Explorer. Mitch popped off a round and then BagDog was gone, out the door on the other side. Venus was after him and Pete kept screaming at him to follow her, he had Chuck.

They ran toward the parking garage of the Sheraton, made the corner and he couldn't see them. At the concrete wall he heard them running down the inside ramp. He vaulted and halfway down realized it was more of a drop than he was expecting. He twisted his ankle but was right in front of the fugitive.

They collided and then Venus was on top of them. It was a scramble of arms and elbows and legs and grappling for guns and knives before cuffs finally locked around a wrist. Then it was just a hard yank and a knee to the face to end it.

Venus looked like hell, bleeding from her mouth and nose and a dozen scrapes, jeans ripped, pony tail mostly pulled free. Mitch figured he was about the same except for the hair and he couldn't seem to put any weight on his foot.

"That kind of week," she said.

BagDog started bucking again. They watched him roll around on the concrete of the parking garage ramp for a little while. When he finally got his feet underneath him and stood, they swooped in and grabbed his arms.

They walked up the ramp, Mitch more leaning on the fugitive than escorting him. BagDog said, "You okay, Marshal?" Mitch leaned harder.

83

As it turned out, Jet didn't need a ride to his father's house. The older Rask sent a car for him. The driver came to the door. Jet was upstairs at the time, heard talking and stuck his head over the railing.

The driver said, "Tell James I'm ready." The fool goon who had opened the door said, "Ain't no James here. Why don't you tally-ho on out of here?" And the driver walked in. Pushed past two wide eyed gangsters with guns, paused long enough to take in what was left of Trey and the disgusted look on Wiggins's face as he worked at cleaning it up, and then came around to the base of the stairs.

"There you are," said the Driver. "It seems I'm not a moment too soon."

"I need to take a shower," said Jet.

"As you wish." The Driver looked around, nose twitching. "I'll be in the car."

He walked out, pausing only to suggest that Wiggins use a mixture of Era Plus detergent and lye on Trey.

Jet took a long shower, partly to clear his head and partly to make the Driver wait. Everyone who worked for his father looked down on him and he didn't like it. They should respect him. He was Jet Rask. He owned people.

84

The Chief came to the hospital to see Chuck. He found Pete and Venus in the room with Sharita. She was not happy. Chuck was in and out of consciousness from the pain killers. Pete gave him the rundown.

Chief put his hand on Sharita's shoulder. "Whatever you need." She thanked him.

Outside the room he ran into Mitch with a cardboard carry tray of coffees. He walked with a distinct limp but had stopped wincing an hour before.

"You all need to take it easy the rest of the week," said Chief.

"Crime doesn't stop just because Venus broke a nail."

Chief was being serious. "It doesn't stop when you arrest a punk like BagDog either. Give it a rest."

Mitch looked at the door to the hospital room. "It shouldn't have happened like that. We've done that move dozens of times. Nobody ever slips the pin."

"Times change," said Chief. "You either change with them or get run over."

"It's just a bad week."

The chief shook his head, clapped Mitch on the shoulder on his way by and said, "Take a break."

85

Pete went home that night and had a very serious conversation with Patti. "I don't like that you do this," she said.

He nodded. "I know."

"I don't think you do. I have not ever liked this. I put up with it because it is what you do and I know that Mitch and Venus won't let anything happen to you but they can't keep you safe, not really, and I don't like this."

"I get it, Baby." He hugged her and she let him. But she didn't stop talking.

"You are a father. It is not just me that you will leave alone."

"I won't leave you alone." He meant it. She could hear it.

"Don't make a promise you can't keep."

"I quit the squad."

She pushed him away, looked at him with her head kind of sideways. He pursed his lips, not a smile or frown. "I told you, I get it."

She threw her arms around him and squealed. "I love you so much."

"Feel like taking a road trip?" he asked. "Chief gave me some admin days if we want to take a long weekend to go house hunting."

86

On Thursday, Kurt Cunningham decided that he'd been waiting long enough. His case was strong and every minute he spent waiting for the SAC to get back from vacation was a minute that the Rask empire was expanding, absorbing legitimate businesses and converting them into minions.

He did some research. Called in a favor from Kim over at the Comm Center. Then he put his briefing book on the front passenger seat of his two year old Fusion and headed toward the shore.

Desperate times call for desperate measures and nobody was more desperate than he was. James Reginald Burton the third had rented a house along Sea View Boulevard for his current wife, her two grown children, his grown child and two younger children, the middle schooler they had together before they were together, and his mother-in-law. They could see the sea. It was not usually relaxing until the third Pina Colada, but it was better than being in the office.

In fact, not being in the office was what made it worth-while. Kurt didn't know that was how James Reginald felt. He was under the impression that the SAC was a man of action, swift justice, and 23 hour work days.

The crash of reality was abrupt and violent. Kurt didn't really know what had happened but gathered that his briefing book had been thrown with great force because he was chasing pages across the dunes and getting dirty looks from people who were convinced he was destroying the only nesting place of the very last sea turtle. Ever.

Kurt didn't mind though. The only intelligible words SAC Burton had uttered were music to his ears. "I don't care what the hell you do. If you can get a judge to sign them, good on you."

Kurt could do that. He knew judges. He could get arrest warrants. Raj had made that certain. All those charts and tables and accounts. Judges ate that stuff up.

He fished a page from some tall dune grasses and noticed a small hole dug into the sand. He looked closer and saw the eggs of a sea turtle. He waved to some of the folks on the beach, said, "Over here. A whole nest of them." They were not appreciative.

87

Kate walked into her chambers and saw Cindy keeping watch over Ramon and FBI Special Agent Kurt Cunningham. Both men stood when she entered. Kurt wouldn't meet her eye.

"Good afternoon, Judge," said Ramon. "I was hoping you would be able to discuss the Harwood matter."

"We already have." She didn't slow down and made a follow-me gesture to Cindy.

"Even so, Judge."

Kurt cleared his throat. "I know you are busy. This will only take a few minutes. I've got some arrest warrants for you to sign."

Kate stopped and looked at him. "Arrest warrants?" He nodded. "Okay, come on in."

Kurt followed her, feeling the weight of destiny on his shoulders and not the seething look from Restrepo.

Kate shut the door behind them and gestured to a chair in front of her desk. Kurt waited until she was behind her desk before taking the seat.

"How is your wife?" asked Kate, smiling.

He flushed in a most adorable way. "Sorry about all of that."

"Water under the bridge. What do you have?"

Kurt told her. Gave her the briefing book.

"Some of the pages are wet."

He said, "There's sand too. The binder opened when Special Agent in Charge Burton was looking at it. I had to chase them down."

She nodded. "I'll get back to you with any questions. Obviously you want to move on this so I'll try to get through it as quickly as I can."

"I appreciate that," he said. "I'd like to put the major players in custody before we start with the grand jury."

"Of course." She showed him out. Ramon still waiting.

"That was quite a stack of warrants," Ramon said to Kurt.

"It's quite a case. Should be good business for you." Kurt laughed at his bad lawyer joke, missed Ramon wince.

"Glad to know we're all working together on this." He shook Kurt's hand and promptly dismissed him. All attention now on the lovely Katherine Silver.

"Is it my turn yet, your Honor?" He was actually charming when he said it and she relented, gesturing into her office. But when he went inside she mouthed, "Thirty minutes," to Cindy.

Half an hour later Ramon left because she received a very important phone call.

88

Mitch and Venus sat in a booth at Vinny's, a half-eaten pepperoni pie between them. Mitch sipped his third beer, she was on her second diet coke.

They got a few looks walking in. Venus's face had exploded in splotches of yellow-brown and her nose was still swollen. Friday night, man and battered woman walk into a place, people make assumptions.

Now, an hour at the table and no raised voices, they were just another couple. Quiet, just with some problems and who didn't have problems?

"Quit brooding," she said. "You're bringing me down."

"Sorry." He drank. Hardly a reassuring sign he was going to snap out of it.

"I mean it." She leaned back. Full or finished, didn't matter which. "You want to tell me this is about Chuck getting hurt, fine. You want to say it's about Pete leaving, sure thing, makes sense. But it's not, is it?"

"It's something like that."

"Nothing like that. You're upset about the girl."

"Why do you hate her so much?" Mitch didn't want to talk about it.

"Why are you upset that it didn't go anywhere?" Venus wasn't big on answering personal questions.

"Because she made me realize how unhappy I was."

Venus shook her head. "You think being with her would make you happy?"

He shrugged. "Not what I said." He went for the beer again. "You ever been with somebody who makes you realize you're missing something?"

"Yes."

"Then you understand." He debated another slice. Decided against it. "I see Pete leaving and I realize he's changed. He's going after something different. He's going to have a family and a house on a lake and probably learn how to fish. He's going to be a boss, responsible and totally different from what he's doing now and he's going to love it and be good at it because he can be more than what he is now."

"You want to be a supervisor?"

' Mitch shook his head. "The street is my life. You know that. It's all that matters."

"Until now."

He met her gaze. "So maybe now I want something else too."

"That's good. You've been a long time coming around." She leaned forward. "Just not at work, right? That's the rule."

"Yeah, that's the rule." He smiled at her. "Thanks."

She signaled to the waiter for the check. "Any time." The man was an ass. Mitch, not the waiter. The waiter was actually kind of cute.

89

Kurt scrambled but couldn't get everything together before the weekend. Terry told him to relax. Rask wasn't going anywhere. They went to see Raj.

The FBI had set Raj and his family up in a rented house about an hour away. It was bourgeois and Connie was disappointed but Raj had come from worse and thought any place that came with guards armed with machine guns was better than being on their own.

The girls complained and stuck up their noses until the TV came on, then they were chill. Connie had questions about cooking and cleaning. When they told her that was her department, she asked who was paying for the takeout. The GS-13s looked at her thousand dollar outfit, million dollar sneer, and chose not to answer. The GS-14 who ran the detail said, "Tell us what you want and we'll make the call. We'll also answer the door. The rest is up to you."

Connie had a few things to say but Raj cut her off and thanked the nice agents. The private conversation between husband and wife was held in a room with paper-thin walls at a volume that would have impressed Spinal Tap.

The official entry in the detail logbook stated, "Subject's family exhibiting difficulty adjusting to protection." That was fair. Characterizing Connie Rasheed as a snob was not. She was scared and the lower-middle class housing was an easy target, the agents on scene the only audience.

She and Raj were on the same page when it came to Jet and they were both terrified. She even apologized to the GS-14 before shift change.

When they found it, afterward, the log book only showed positive entries for the rest of the detail.

90

In much the same way that in a town with two streets one is Main and the other is Washington something, in any government office suite with two conference rooms, one of them is always called, "the large conference room." Kurt and Terry moved base camp into the large conference room of the U. S. Attorney's Office. It was a long room with a heavy wood table, comfortable reclining high-backed chairs, a twisting spider plant of a speaker phone system, video teleconference camera, and two large television screens. The room was huge, easily seating 24 people with enough space to put their elbows on the table.

Big as it was, there was standing room only. Men, and the occasional woman, all dressed impeccably in off-the-rack business attire, waited breathlessly for the announcement of the plan. The U. S. Attorney himself was there to say a few words. Then Reginald James Burton, Special Agent in Charge, said a few more words. They weren't as coherent, but did manage to convey the idea of patriotism and hard work and it being a great day for America's premiere law enforcement agency.

By that point, everyone was so tired of off-the-cuff that Kurt's three inch briefing book was a relief. The lights dimmed and the screens brought up a PowerPoint title slide. It read, "The Plan to Capture David Rask by Federal Bureau of Investigation Special Agent Kurt Cunningham."

The next slide had his contact information. The next slide listed Terry Gaff's Bona fides. Off-the-cuff found itself back in style.

Eventually Terry jumped in. "The Rask organization has been trafficking a variety of illegal goods for years, from stolen intellectual property on the tech side to living flesh and blood with their slavery product line. When the son, James "Jet" Rask returned from college, he brought in extortion and distribution of illegal narcotics." Terry looked around the room. "Today all of that will stop."

He picked up a stack of papers and flipped through them. "Judge Silver signed these arrest warrants less than 72 hours ago." Terry rifled through the stack and pulled one out specifically. "Including this one, for David Rask himself."

There was a collective intake of breath. David was a big fish, politically connected and hard to keep crosshairs on. That was a ballsy warrant and one that Gaff and Cunningham better be able to backup or their careers were over.

Kurt stepped back in. "You all are team leaders. Each of you has a briefing packet that I'd like you to share with your team when we clear here."

An image of David Rask playing tennis appeared on the screens. "Our main target is this man. David Rask. He's the head and most definitely the brains."

The screen changed to show Jet posing beside his Hummer, Wiggins and Trey in the background lending gangster cred to his image. At the bottom of the image was a tagline crediting the image to www.bootyislandpirateking.com.

Kurt said, "However, this man is responsible for the spike in violence associated with the organization and is the more aggressive of the two. Watch your back."

Kurt advanced to a slide showing a graphic picture of a murder scene, corpses littered with bullet wounds and copious amounts of blood. The more dainty agents turned away. "Jet should be considered extremely dangerous. He is armed, travels with armed escort, and is the lead suspect in a half dozen gangland murder cases."

Kurt looked around the room, serious as a politician telling you that taxes have to come down, "Witnesses say the man, someone they didn't see clearly enough to identify as Jet when they were on the stand, had guns pointed at him but drew without hesitation, from concealment." Kurt snapped but it was sort of a dud. He clapped, somebody jumped. "That fast. No fear."

Gaff stepped back in. "This is a higher tech crew than you are used to. They're spoofing their phones, have wireless video surveillance, and can probably intercept your mobile data traffic. Use encrypted channels on the radios instead of your phones and stick to the timeline. Anybody gets hit early it will blow the whole operation."

"Or late," said Kurt. "If you're late you'll miss your man."

"Or late," agreed Gaff.

The meeting broke up with Kurt handing out the briefing packets like they were diplomas. A couple of agents traded. There was too much chit chat for anyone to hear Kurt say, "Be careful out there." But he said it anyway.

91

There are a lot of cops who will tell you that 'careful' is their middle name. None of them was on the SWAT team that jog-walked from the PD's ready room to the parking garage and split off into three columns with the precision of a water ballet team. The first stringers swung up into their panel truck. Another team took the armored car. The rookies, in all their bench warming glory, boarded the Chevy Express extended wheelbase 18 passenger van. Those SWAT guys, if they bothered to talk to you at all, would say their middle names were Colt or Remington or Badass. Then they would tell you they deployed under the cover of the garage so that the skulls on the street wouldn't know they were coming.

SWAT was hard core. Armed and armored with the finest that the city council's funding cuts could provide. The three vehicles raced out to the street, emergency lights flashing, city seal and PD moniker proudly displayed under giant block letters that spelled SWAT.

92

The News Channel 14, Live at 3:30 (the only station that gives you 8 hours of continuous local news) chopper caught one of the arrests. It was the perfect blend of style and substance, a made for the screen real-life oh-yeah climax, all the excitement of Michael Bay without the explosions.

Two marked squad cars boxed a pearl Escalade and when it pulled to the side of the road, a black suburban screeched into the frame. Agents in suits with guns in their hands leaped out and pulled bandits from the Caddy.

A bit of turbulence caused the camera to shift during the part where the FBI guys borrowed handcuffs from the local officers.

Just down the street, three uniformed officers followed two FBI agents, one in a grey pinstripe and the other in a very fresh black on black hound's-tooth, up the stoop of a row house.

They pounded on the door for a few minutes then went in. It smelled like death with bad breath. Grease streaked the walls and piles from the dog covered the floor. Boxes filled with everything from ab rollers to plastic toys leaned haphazardly against the walls and each other. Clothes and dishes covered nearly every surface.

The backdoor slammed as they went in. One of the PD guys started to run toward it but the G-Man held out an arm. "Ops plan says we start here and work our way back. Don't want to miss anything."

The cops exchanged looks, the kind that said, how can you be so dumb and still get paid so much money? Then the first cop keyed his radio mic and said, "Team 12 negative results. Subject exited rear of address on foot, unknown direction of travel."

Pinstripe nodded. "That's a good idea. They might see him on the street while we finish up here."

Third cop said, "I'll be in the car."

93

Three black Suburbans, windows tinted and no decals, tore up the driveway that lead to the Rask mansion. Special Agent Kurt Cunningham was out the door of the lead truck before it even stopped, Robert Something-or-other at his heels. Behind them the FBI's crack H.R.T. (and these guys would tell you their middle names were Careful) kitted out in full tactical, deployed around the perimeter.

When the team was in place, Kurt rang the doorbell. He waited. Was about to ring it again when it opened, quietly, revealing soft light and an immaculate foyer.

The Butler stood in the doorway, his finely tailored suit putting the younger men's to shame. "Good evening," he said. "May I help you?"

Kurt flashed his creds in the old man's face. "FBI, step aside."

"You can't do that," said the Butler even as Kurt rudely pushed him out of the way. He brushed his lapel smooth and then took the paper offered by Robert-something-or-other. Half of the tactical team followed them inside.

Kurt paused once he entered and turned a slow, awe-struck circle. The house was huge inside, opulent in a way he'd only seen on PBS. The grand staircase rose to an upstairs that was just as nice. There were so many doors and rooms he had no idea where to go.

Kurt walked over to where the Butler read the arrest warrant. "We're here to see your boss."

"I see that, Sir."

"You need to take us to him," said Kurt.

"He is not currently receiving visitors." The Butler frowned at them over the top of the warrant. Kurt looked meaningfully at the Tactical team. The Butler caught his drift, walked down the hallway. "But you will find him in the library, this way."

The agents followed. It was a stately and respectable walk, a pace that allowed them to appreciate the antique French furniture as much as possible, considering they had no idea what any of the pieces was actually worth.

Except Robert Something-or-other who stopped beside a bench and whistled. "Is this original?" he asked the Butler.

"It is, Sir," said the Butler, smiling. "Everything here is."

They reached a door at the end of the hall that lead into the library. The Butler knocked twice then opened it and said, "Good evening, Sir. The FBI to see you."

The Butler faded into the background when Kurt and the other agents swept into the room. It was a place of dark wood and books, built for brandy and cigars. A handful of table top statues lived on shelves and end tables and there was a silver tray with crystal decanters on a buffet table. Oriental carpets covered parquet flooring, a chandelier cast soft light over the entire room, floor lamps sat beside the various wing back chairs and couches, upholstered in dark red leather.

David Rask sat on a couch, a lit cigar in his hand, a book in his lap, and a snifter of brandy on a crystal coaster nearby. He was dressed casually and obviously hadn't quite processed what the Butler had said. Ginger was across from him, in sweats with her legs pulled up on a chaise and a paperback laid flat against her chest. She looked hungry, staring at the men in their body armor with slung M-4 carbines at hand.

"David Rask," said Kurt, "You are under arrest."

Rask laughed, took a sip of his brandy. He set the glass down and his features turned hard and cold. He was more terrifying than Jet could ever be but usually kept it hidden. "I don't know who you are, but I will find out. Nobody comes into my house-"

"Stand up and put your hands behind your-"

"Disrespects me like this. You will be sorry."

Kurt had cuffs in his hand. "Maybe you haven't been keeping up on current events here? The FBI is arresting you. Get up and turn around."

Rask said, "Cuffs? You really don't know what's going on here." He stood but did not offer his hands. "I'm a pillar of this community. I'm not going to run away from you or fight you in your little police car."

Kurt didn't budge. Rask leaned close. "When you are dumb enough to arrest a man like me you call first, and tell me when I should come to your station, and then I show up. You don't pull a stunt like this unless you want to lose your job." He waved, gesturing at the men tracking dirt into his library.

Kurt grabbed the hand when it went by his face, snapped on the cuff and twisted Rask around. He pushed him forward, struggling for the second hand. David hit the back of the couch and went over. Kurt fell into him hard and knocked the wind out of the older man. The second cuff went on. "I don't think you understand how this works. You're going down for the count this time."

Ginger was wide eyed, almost panting, excited by what was happening. She tried to struggle a little bit, just to keep things interesting, but the agents were too strong. It wasn't nearly as much fun as she'd hoped.

David was furious. "Do you have any idea who I am?"

Kurt stared back at him, unflinching. "I know exactly who you are. That's why I said, David Rask, you're under arrest."

Rask chuckled. "Okay then, we'll see how this goes." Kurt jerked his handcuffs, pulled him out of the room. Nearly every FBI agent has an arrest during his career and for Kurt, this one was a wet dream come true.

Rask called over his shoulder to the butler as he was dragged down the hallway. "You know whom to call."

"Of course, Sir." Like this sort of thing happened every day. He escorted them all to the door, made sure it was shut behind them, then made the call.

When he was finished with the phone, he went to a door hidden at the base of the staircase and took out a broom and dustpan. The FBI had tracked in dirt from their stroll through the garden and it was driving him crazy.

94

Jet's meeting with his father had not gone well. Jet stormed out swearing he'd never speak to the old man again, which suited them both just fine. Thing of it was, Jet still hid out at the lake house waiting for the okay to head back into town.

Wiggins was able to get him to the club one night but he was such a nervous wreck, convinced that his father, or worse yet, Ginger, would see him that he spent most of the evening in his truck. He only made a brief foray into his office to check on the contents of his hidden safes.

A police detective had come around the house a little before 9 which was the official wake-up time of Jet's crew. He was responding to a complaint from some families about things that may have happened to their daughters while at one of Jet's parties.

It took a little while for the hungover gangsters to get their bearings, and then find their boss, during which time the nice policeman was able to observe the inside of the house. Of particular note was the strong smell of marijuana, the guns sticking out of cushions and sitting on end tables (presumably unregistered considering the situation), and most interesting of all, a carpet stain that looked suspiciously like a place where someone was shot to death.

Jet came down the stairs about the time the detective found the bullet holes in the wall. "What can I do you for officer?" He said it as two questions, the first was why are you here and the second who are you?

The policeman produced a credential case from the breast pocket of his tan herringbone blazer and showed off his badge. "Detective Sergeant Willis, BCI."

Jet was disappointed he wasn't a marshal, or even the FBI, but at least he was state. "Nice to meet you. Door's that way." He pointed.

"Thanks, I got a little disoriented, what with the size of this place and all the smoke." He looked around but didn't walk toward the door. "I'm here about a party. Looks like it was a doozy."

Jet reached the bottom of the stairs. "Yeah, you're just a bit too late. Everybody left a couple of days ago."

"Shame." Willis walked over to the wall with the bullet holes, noted that there were still slugs in it. "Got anything to eat? I've suddenly got the munchies."

Jet nodded to Wiggins who produced a can of salted peanuts. "We'll keep it down next time, Detective. Promise."

Willis took a handful of nuts. He actually felt kind of hungry. On his way to the door he said, "You should probably open a window."

"Good idea." Jet walked with him. His head hurt. Wasn't nearly as cool as he played it.

At the door Detective Willis turned, still the nice policeman. "Couldn't help but notice those holes in your wall."

Jet laughed, a big, deep, fake laugh. "We were playing a drinking game and one of the guys fired off a few rounds."

"The weapon still here?"

"Naw, it was one of the guests. Probably the guy who called you." Jet smiled, tried to be reassuring. Looked more like a defense attorney.

"Probably," agreed Willis, nodding his head. "Thanks for the nuts."

"Anytime." Jet shut the door behind him. Turned, cold rage warring with pounding headache. "Which one of you idiots let him in here?"

What followed was a morning of finger pointing and then an afternoon of planning with Jet ultimately calling his father in the early evening. He got the Butler. Then he got the news. Shared his own adventure with the BCI guy in a state of shock. Butler said, "Get out. Go far and quiet. I'll call when it's clear."

Jet didn't argue. He knew this time it was bad. They got the crew together and headed into town. Wiggins called Lonnie at the club. Lonnie said, "I'll call you back from outside."

Lonnie climbed into the passenger seat of Big Maggie's Caprice. She'd started letting him borrow it to go to work because he always left the tank full and she didn't like him walking home that late. He dialed Wiggins.

"We're coming in for some traveling money," said Wiggins.

"You going to hang for a bit? Club's really hopping tonight." Lonnie noticed a dark SUV on the corner of the block. He tried to remember if it was there when he'd gone out to the dumpster earlier.

"No time. We're getting out of town. I think there's some heat on us."

Lonnie spotted a man standing at the bus stop. Not the sort of man who usually rode the bus from around here. "You might want to wave off completely then."

Wiggins didn't like that. "Man needs cash."

"I think that's a bad idea." Lonnie could hear bits of the conversation between Wiggins and Jet. "Maybe it's nothing, just don't pull up in the Hummer."

Wiggins said, "It's what we've got."

Lonnie decided the man was definitely not waiting for the bus. "You guys get out. I'm telling you, that Hummer rolls in and everybody in it is going to be taken."

"Problem is the cash," said Wiggins.

"Get out, send in the Hummer. If nothing happens? Great, come get the cash. But if he gets taken, you don't need the cash that bad."

"I'll call you back," said Wiggins.

From the FBI's perspective, the take down of Jet's crew at Booty Island was a bit more dramatic and had better choreography than the Rask mansion, even if they did have to stake it out for a couple of extra nights. The club was in a seedy section of the city, at the end of street where most of the lights were out. Pools of neon lit the front of the building, flashing palm trees and treasure chests washed the patrons in multicolored hues, but the rest of the block was dark. A line of gangsters and their girlfriends stood outside the entrance, inching along the line between pools of light and shadow then back again on their way to the door.

Dance music thumped through the night, louder when the club's doors opened. Jet's Hummer crept along the street and agents moved swiftly to intercept it. It was one of those things, a decision had to be made and the man with tactical command made it. No Jet, but now the location was blown it was time to take down the club.

"GO. GO. GO."

Agents swarmed from vans and abandoned buildings, converged on the club. FBI, HRT, and SWAT reflected from big letters on the backs of their vests, M-4 carbines in their hands. All business. The crowd parted. Then dispersed.

The PD paddy wagon rolled up and more officers jumped out, grabbing anyone still within reach. Inside, the bouncers were overwhelmed and cuffed. The cops moved around the dance floor and took control. A team headed up the stairs and when they breached the door at the top, the downstairs crew took the DJ booth and the club went silent. Lights came up and even the most stoned of the patrons realized the party was over.

In the private office upstairs, three of Jet's toughs were putting the moves on a young woman, lured from downstairs by the promise of wealth and mixed nuts. The FBI wasted no time cuffing them all. No sign of Jet. Even under the couch.

"Where's Rask?" asked the FBI. The agent had his foot on the thug's head and the barrel of his rifle against the man's temple.

"Easy, I got no beef," said the gangster. "Jet's working."

"What do you mean?" FBI wanted real information.

"His old man sent him up north or something. Told him to get out of town." The thug tried to move but was pinned.

"Doing what?"

"I can't think with your foot on my head."

The FBI moved. "What about now?"

"I don't know what he's doing." The thug looked around. "He hired a new manager and then took off. I haven't seen him in weeks. Wiggins says he's doing something important."

"Who is Wiggins?"

"Who is what?" asked the thug just before the boot moved back to his head.

95

Lonnie saw Jet's white Hummer drive between the dark SUV and the man at the bus stop. Cops erupted from everywhere and took the truck before it even reached the parking lot.

Lonnie's cell phone rang. It was Wiggins. Lonnie said, "They got your man."

Wiggins was not in a good mood. "Get us something."

Lonnie watched SWAT roll on the club. He jumped at a knock on his window. There was a cop there, motioning him out. He raised a finger, and pointed at the phone. "Listen, cop telling me I got to go. Check the dumpster when they clear. It isn't much but it'll get you out of town."

The door was opened for him and he was assisted out and then against the hood of the car. He protested, said he was a working man, but they weren't taking any chances, and Lonnie was added to the parade of former patrons in flex cuffs.

96

Mitch asked Cindy to ask Kate about maybe having dinner. Kate told Cindy to tell Mitch that she didn't want to go out. Mitch asked about eating in and Kate thought that would be okay, but not at her place since she didn't have any groceries yet.

That small concession brought Mitch back from the mood he'd been in. Kate texted him in the early afternoon asking for his address. "I've got a car now. I can drive myself."

He gave it to her. She arrived promptly at seven. He was still prepping so she washed up and jumped in to help. It gave them something easy to talk about while the first glass of Mosel Riesling got to work.

Kate was nervous and rambled as she chopped. "So any way, Rask has two attorneys helping Restrepo, both from New York, and they are filing every sort of motion imaginable and objecting every three seconds during the proceedings. It's a little intimidating."

"Weren't you the same way when you were a trial attorney?" said Mitch.

Kate snorted. She was glad he'd called. Glad she'd got over stubborn just enough to accept.

"Defense attorneys are idiots. You can handle them," said Mitch.

"Thanks," she said. "It's just these guys, they're pretty high priced idiots who really know the law."

"Does it remind you why you left New York?"

Kate said, "That's funny."

She started to cut an onion. Mitch walked over, "You're doing it wrong."

"So now you know how to be a judge too?" said Kate, suddenly defensive. Mitch put his hand on hers to stop her from cutting any more. She froze, the battle inside her over Mitch resumed.

"No, the onion." They were close. She leaned back a little, into him, but just to see him clearly.

She said, "I didn't realize there was a right way."

"There's a right way for everything." His voice was deep and quiet. They looked at each other.

"Show me." There was a moment when anything could have happened. It was why they couldn't do this and why they both wanted to anyway. But it passed.

Mitch took the knife from her, cut the onion in half lengthwise. He laid it flat and sliced neatly several times, parallel to the counter, leaving the slices attached to the stem. She watched, intrigued. At the top he stopped, then sliced again, at angles from one side to the other, again leaving the slices attached. Finally he held it firmly and chopped from the end to the stem, perfectly sized pieces fell free from the sharp blade.

He gave her back the knife. She took a breath, then duplicated what he did on the other half of the onion. It didn't come out quite right, but it was close.

"She slices, she dices." He smiled. There was another moment. "Why did you leave New York?"

"I wanted to be a judge, the opening was here," she said. He reached for the bottle of wine and topped off their glasses.

"In vino veritas."

Kate looked at the onion, layers chopped expertly by the man next to her pretending to know Latin. "I was spinning my wheels, getting nowhere, doing nothing." She sipped the wine.

"You wanted more." He nodded.

"I wanted different," she said. "I spent six years engaged to a man who was already married."

Mitch was surprised. Kate went on, "To his job. And so was I. We both worked crazy hours because we said the law was everything. Sometimes we'd go weeks without seeing each other." Mitch understood that, watched as she took another sip.

"But it was empty," said Kate. She looked out the window. "We were both hiding from that truth, despite plenty of vino."
She smiled.

"So now you're hiding here?" asked Mitch.

Her smile scrunched into a friendly scowl. "You sure know how to woo a lady."

Mitch turned back to the steak. "I think this is about ready for the fire."

Katherine caught something, more than just moving along. His eyes were frightened. "Wait a minute. I just dumped a six year engagement on you and you want to put a steak on the fire?"

"A man's got to eat." He smiled at her but she wasn't going to let go that easily.

She handed him the wine. "In vino veritas."

"What is this?" he asked. "Truth or dare?"

Kate said, "You started it." She was friendly but aggressive. "And more like truth or truth."

Mitch took the glass, debating something inside. He drank half of the wine in a single gulp. "I don't know what I think about your engagement. I don't know what I think about you. I don't know what you are even doing here." It came out in a rush and now it wouldn't stop.

"It's been years since a woman was in this kitchen." He caught her looking at the onion. "I've never taught anyone how to cut an onion. I feel like I should say something profound about layers but I'm not like that."

She considered what he said, let it wash over her. When she finally answered, it was quiet and gentle. "I don't know what I'm doing here either, but thank you." Their eyes stayed together, searching but not expecting anything. Then she gestured to the onion. "I've been doing it wrong my whole life."

"You're welcome," said Mitch.

The time wasn't right for more. She brushed her face with her hands then grabbed the steak and headed to the deck. He watched her, feeling everything, then scooped up the glasses and followed.

97

The Grand Prix Motor Lodge may have seen better days before anyone named Bush was president but it was unlikely. Some places are built seedy and although worn, the original high pile carpet had that look. So did the stained wallpaper, its green and white stripes faded to nearly the same color.

Jet paced, cramped between the door and the first of two lumps that passed for double beds. Wiggins was sprawled out on one, watching TV, doing his best to ignore Jet. Three other men sat on the edge of the second bed. They didn't look like the sort to watch news but that, and a couple of shopping networks, were the only channels on tap.

The lead story circled around and Jet stopped, his shirt half untucked and pants a wrinkled mess, to watch. He had one of his pistols in his hand and kept raising it toward the newscaster. The big man on the small screen was primped quite well, thank you, and delivered his report about the collapse of the Rask Cartel with the same excitement he usually used to describe blizzards, fires, and fatal car accidents.

"This is unreal," said Jet. "Can you believe this?" None of them could. David Rask was visible in a grainy night shot, probably from a cell phone, being escorted from his mansion into the back of an unmarked SUV. "I can't believe it." He shook his head. "Unreal."

Wiggins eyed the door behind Jet. Noticed sweat beading on his boss's brow and his fingers were completely white where they gripped the pistol.

Jet gestured again at the screen, now showing Ginger being escorted out. "That's my mother. They can't lock up my mother."

"It's okay," said Wiggins. "Mr. Rask will set them straight."

Jet turned on him. "Not this time. I promised he wouldn't go to jail." A drop of spittle hung on his cheek. Wiggins stared at it, afraid to move.

"We need to get all our guys," said Jet, pacing again. "All our guys who aren't in jail. We need to get them and start going after people until this is fixed. That's what we need to do. This is unreal."

The three men looked at Wiggins for direction. Wiggins kept his eye on Jet's pistol.

Jet said, "I want you to find Rasheed. I want you take him out. Take his family out. Burn his house. Destroy everything he ever got from my family."

Wiggins nodded, agreeing, said, "Only problem is that the FBI has him."

Jet stopped. Looked sweetly at Wiggins, spoke as if to a child, "Then find out where they are hiding him. If he's dead, he can't testify and then they will release my father."

"We may have to go outside for help," said Wiggins. "I think they scooped up the rest of the crew. You saw what happened at the club."

Jet nodded, "Whatever." He turned back to the door, then spun. "And," he was very dramatic, "I want my Hummer back."

98

Chief leaned against the wall in the warrants office. He'd taken his tie off already, was on his way out the door and had come back. Mitch sat in his chair, unhappy.

"You want my badge and gun?" he asked.

Chief shook his head. "It's a suspension, not a termination. Not now, anyway. Just leave your keys."

Mitch stood, pulled his keys out from down deep. "You know this is bull."

"You broke her wrist."

Mitch shook his head. "She had a house full of weed and resisted. I can't help it if she's got osteoporosis."

Chief stepped over, put his hand on Mitch's shoulder. "Son, it doesn't matter that she was dealing, or that you got your man because she called him from the hospital." He looked out the window. "There are rules. And we all have to follow them."

Mitch laughed. "Is this where you tell me that you don't want to do this but headquarters is making you?"

Chief walked to the door. Turned, "Nope."

99

Jet didn't want to be left alone, Wiggins said he couldn't get Rasheed by himself. They compromised and took everybody. Wiggins wasn't pleased.

"You need to chill, Boss," he said. Jet glowered, fondled his 45. "At least put that thing away."

Jet did. "I want my Hummer first."

Wiggins nodded. It was in the police impound lot on the west end of town. The lot looked more like a junk yard than a parking lot and there was only a single rent-a-cop at the gate. Wiggins offered to pay the man but Jet was in a hurry, no time to make a deal, and shot him.

They had to hotwire the truck, after they broke out one of the rear windows. Fortunately one of the guys had been a booster before he started working for Jet. "Hummers are easy," he said.

Once they were in and driving, Jet seemed to settle down. Until he discovered the can of nuts was gone. They stopped at a CVS and this time Wiggins was able to make a deal without any gunplay.

One of the guys waited for him outside the truck. "I'm getting worried about the boss," he said. Wiggins told him to shut up and get back in.

They broke into Rasheed's house and had fun smashing things. They made a big pile in the middle of the basement and spent 20 minutes looking for gas before giving up and piling on all of Mrs. Rasheed's candles.

They watched long enough to make sure the house was engaged before driving away, the fire cast shadows inside the Hummer.

"That felt good," said Jet. "Let's get some blow and party."

Wiggins dropped him off at a hotel, left the guys. "You keep your head down, Boss. I'll go find Rasheed."

Wiggins was tempted to run but he didn't have any money left. They'd used his stash to get away when they couldn't get to Booty Island. He needed to see this through. Then Jet would owe him and he'd take it all. Maybe even put a bullet in his head just because.

But at that moment he had a different problem. He had to scare up Rasheed's location. His first stop was an all-night drug store where he bought foot powder and envelopes. His last stop was the lobby of the Central Post Office where he bought a hundred dollars' worth of stamps and mailed his letters.

100

Mitch sat on his couch, flipped through the channels and tried to keep a light buzz going. He kept looking at his phone, wondering if he should call Kate. If she would answer. If it would make anything better.

He woke up at 2 am with a stiff neck and the start of headache and went to bed. Maybe tomorrow.

When it was tomorrow he didn't call. He'd slept late and when he got around to finding his phone it was nearly ten. He had a text from Kate, expressing shock he was suspended. "Don't call me," she'd said. "You aren't who I thought you were."

He kind of felt the same way.

101

Terry Gaff sat at the desk in his office and absently sifted through his mail. His attention was on the TV news report of Rasheed's house burning down and he was concerned. He picked up an envelope addressed by hand with way too many stamps and opened it, eyes on the TV.

He pulled out a single sheet of paper and a lot of white powder. That got his attention and he scrambled for the phone.

"It's Gaff," he said. "I've got a white powder letter in my office."

He hung up, waited, sweat a bit. His eyes fell across the letter. Neat block print said, "Your witness is burning. Release David Rask or you will too."

102

The small conference room in the U.S. Attorney's office had been sanitized of Rask case material but Kurt and Terry were still there. So was Steve Hart and a collection of envelopes and single page letters.

Steve said, "Both of you, Judge Silver, a congressman, and the Sheriff received these letters with the same powder. Our headquarters has opened a protective investigation and we'll keep you apprised."

"Comforting," said Gaff.

"It is just foot powder," said Steve. "Happens all the time."

"It's Jet," said Kurt.

Steve nodded. "Probably."

"So there's nothing to investigate. He got mad and sent some letters. It's the tool of someone who is powerless."

A cell phone rang. They all checked. It was Kurt's and he answered it.

Kurt's expression of scorn changed to surprise, then anger, and out of nowhere came a man of action, a voice of command, the cop he always thought he was and nobody expected him to be. "Move Rasheed and his family. Between the letters and the house, Jet is still in play and we have to assume they've been compromised."

He hung up. "Neighbors described a white Hummer speeding away from the Rasheed blaze."

Terry shook his head. "I thought his car was impounded."

"It was," said Kurt. "Until Jet shot the man guarding it. I'll have the video for you for the trial."

"If you have Jet," said Steve.

"It's just a matter of time." Kurt's mind swarmed with ideas. "He'll make a mistake and we'll get him."

"Why don't you just release the warrant so we can pick him up?" asked Steve. "Before somebody else gets hurt."

Kurt laughed at him. "You think I'm going to give this to the marshals? My big case, a gift to you wrapped up with a bow? Forget about it." (He didn't pull off the 'forget about it,' it sounded pretty lame.) "We'll catch him."

Steve looked at Terry for support but the AUSA was busy typing an email on his phone. Kurt said, "Tell you what, when I do have him in custody I'll let your guys haul him to jail."

103

A black Suburban with heavily tinted windows pulled up to the safe
house that held the Rasheed family. The only thing that might have stood out to
the casual observer was that it backed into the driveway and when the passenger
got out, in a light gray suit and dark sunglasses, the driver stayed behind with
the engine running. A more astute observer, one who knew cars, would note
that the windows looked thick, the door, when it opened, took a lot of effort and
had an extra hinge, and the whole car sat a little lower on tires that were just a
tad too wide.

The agent in the gray suit ran inside. The agent in the Suburban made a
phone call. He didn't spot the white Hummer parked three houses up.

The four men in the Hummer noticed the armored Suburban though.
Jet was in the front passenger seat and held a Bushmaster AR-15. The other
three were the men who had been with him in the hotel, the two in back also had
Bushmasters. A Mac-10 sat beside the driver.

"As soon as they come out, you go," said Jet. The driver nodded. The
toughs were excited. They'd been sitting around for way too long and the
promise of action was intoxicating.

The agent in the gray suit stepped out of the house, a Heckler and Koch
MP-40 slung over his shoulder. He looked up and down the street then
motioned behind him.

"Get ready," said Jet.

A second agent stepped out of the house, also with an MP-40. Gray
suit walked quickly to the Suburban and opened the rear door. The second agent
started forward, Connie and the two girls at his heels. A third agent behind them.
Then Raj. Then another agent.

The Hummer leapt forward, engine roaring, tires squealing, and an
open can of Planter's Party Mix spilling from the dashboard.

The Hummer skidded onto the lawn and the gangsters bailed out, guns
blazing. The agents returned fire, striking Jet's driver. He slumped over the

wheel and the truck crashed into the Suburban, crushed the gray suit and trapped the FBI driver.

Jet fired, calm, and dropped one of the agents. His toughs sprayed everywhere, breaking windows, digging up shrubs, burning through their magazines like it was a race. Connie was hit and the other agent was winged but kept shooting and dropped one of the gangsters.

The other agent sprayed the Hummer from the doorway of the house. Jet dove for cover and reloaded. His man had a jam and knelt in the grass trying to work the action. The wounded agent took him out. Jet finished the agent and tracked on Rasheed who clung to his wife, blood pouring out of her.

Rasheed screamed as soft point .223 rounds tore into him. The agent in the house stepped out, spraying his fresh magazine and Jet rolled off-line. The agent grabbed Rasheed's shirt, dragged him into the house.

Jet came up from his roll firing and caught the agent in the neck. The man stared at him for a moment and collapsed. Screeching metal distracted him and he saw the Suburban backing up.

Jet spun around to the back of his Hummer, reloaded, and came up behind the front wheel, rifle aimed across the hood at the Suburban. He fired and the round smacked against the bullet resistant glass. He fired again. The glass spidered. Another shot. And again. He breached the glass and grazed the agent.

The driver swung open the door and dropped out of the truck, firing at Jet. The shots were wide and Jet didn't flinch. Three more rounds from the AR finished the agent. He walked up the path and looked at the bodies by the house.

Connie was soaked in blood, fading fast. The girls had been torn apart. Raj's body lay half in the house, a fallen agent over him.

Jet loaded his last magazine and walked into the street. A green Honda stopped short. Started to back away but halted when Jet pointed the rifle at the driver.

He walked around to the driver's side and pulled the man out. "You need to call the police," said Jet. "Tell them what happened here."

He got into the car. The man stared at him, horrified and frozen in fear. "Get out your phone, dial 9-1-1 and tell them." The man got out his phone. "Tell them this is what happens when they put my father in jail."

104

Steve Hart and Kurt Cunningham sat across from the Honorable Katherine Silver in her chambers. She was trying very hard to be calm and failing miserably.

"This is a serious threat, Judge," said Steve. "It's more than letters. We're putting a detail on you."

"I can't believe this is really happening," she said.

"Believe it," said Kurt. "It's real. I just lost five agents."

"But why me? What did I do?"

Steve said, "You signed the warrants. Right now you're the only person who stands between David Rask and freedom."

She rearranged a stack of papers on her desk. Fought back tears. Something she hated about herself, strong emotion always brought them out.

"Don't worry," said Kurt. "We'll keep you safe."

The trial attorney came out, her cross-examination glare and tone. "How, exactly, do you plan to do that? You just lost five agents and your star witness."

He didn't have a comeback. Steve answered for him. "We are going to keep you safe. The Marshals Service." He looked at Kurt. "It's what we do."

"How long is this going to last?" asked Katherine.

Steve shrugged. "Probably until Jet is arrested. He seems to be on a rampage right now, I'd be uncomfortable backing off until we know he can't touch you."

"This is crazy," she said.

"I know ma'am, and I'm sorry," said Steve. "We'll be as non-intrusive as possible but we'll have to be with you all the time."

105

Pete stood just outside his open garage and stirred a 10 gallon pot over a heavy duty propane. He wore shorts and his "These are the Good Old Days" t-shirt and was quite content. He had a beer in his other hand.

Behind him, two folding lawn chairs sat in the driveway. One was empty and the other held Mitch, sullen and nursing his own beer. Mitch stared through the fire and steam at the street, Pete's Camaro, and the Harley he'd ridden over on.

Pete said, "Cascade is the way to go." He looked at the bubbling wort, savoring the smell of beer to be. "Some guys use Willamette but that's just flash."

He was relaxed, the Yang to Mitch's Yin. "Of course," he continued, "I think the yeast is more important to the final taste than which hops you use." He sat down.

Mitch, not looking at him, "What the hell?"

Pete felt philosophical, brewing on a summer night with a light buzz, and ignored Mitch. He sat down. "Not everybody likes IPA. It's strong, hoppy." He took a swig. "They aren't like the regular pale ales, all light and flowery. You know why they brewed them that way?"

Mitch kept brooding.

"It's because they had to be tough. Make it all the way from England to India without going bad. Bass just had to ride a few leagues in a wagon to get to a pub. The IPAs went around the world." It was why Pete loved them, why he wanted everyone to love them.

Mitch sipped, still not looking and definitely trying not to listen.

Pete kept on. "Now stout on the other hand, that's a different story altogether."

Mitch threw his beer bottle out into the night. Pete stopped talking, stared after it. "Are you kidding me? I don't care about stout or IPA or your stupid yeast."

Pete stood. Aimless for a minute then he went to the pot and stirred again. "If you don't keep stirring the wort it boils over." He sighed. Kept looking at the night. "I can't do this forever, Mitch."

Mitch stared at his friend's back. He knew the truth of it. Hated the truth. The truth really sucked lately. "We've got a good thing going."

Pete checked his watch then dropped in more hops. "When Karen left me I thought my life was over. She and I, we had a good thing going."

Patti walked into the garage from the house, saw the two men, waited in the open doorway.

Pete said, "It crushed me. You know that?" He stirred, thinking. "I don't want to lose Patti or my kid. I can't keep doing this."

Mitch glared at the pot. Tried to flip it over with his mind. Patti slipped back inside, unseen. Mitch said, "So you're just going to run out."

The spoon stopped. Pete shook his head. "To make beer, good beer, you need ingredients that go together. You have to put them together the right way. You boil them carefully."

He turned off the gas and the flame died. The pot settled.

Mitch said, "And?"

Pete sighed. "And when it's done, you have to take it off the fire."

"That's what you think you're doing?"

Pete sat back down. "The job is not what's important in life." He pointed his thumb at the house behind him. "What's in there is. You think you can sit outside and enjoy a cold one with the job on a summer night?"

Mitch shook his head.

"Of course not," said Pete. "And does the job wrap its arms around you when you go inside and say I love you?"

"I'm not like you."

"You could be," said Pete. "You should be. I saw you and Kate together. Make that work. The rest of this is just garnish."

Mitch raised an eyebrow. "Garnish? You were almost making sense for a minute."

Pete laughed. Mitch said, "She won't talk to me anymore."

"Have you even tried?"

106

Mitch drove away angry. Patti had said goodbye like she wasn't going to see him again and he had the feeling that he wouldn't be back to that house ever. Pete tried to dress things up and said some nice things, but the truth was he was leaving and breaking up the band and it hurt.

He opened up the bike, let the night wash over him and the fresh air clear his head. He kept thinking about Kate, about the job, about losing everything all at once. He was already out, suspended for who knew how long, and it made him realize that at least some of what Pete said was true, the job didn't care about him, wouldn't curl up with him on the couch.

Mind made up, he drove to Kate's house. The detail was just bringing her home so he pulled up to the curb a couple houses down from where the motorcade parked. There was a Mercedes in her driveway. He knew that car. It wasn't hers.

Deputy marshals posted on their lead vehicle. Now that he looked he could see a perimeter patrol too. Something must have happened. Pete hadn't said anything.

He recognized Marci as the deputy-in-charge of the detail, and she opened the door for Kate. He watched her slip out, dressed well, with a doggie bag. Then he saw Ramon climb out behind her. His blood boiled.

Kate waited for Ramon on the curb. Said, "Thank you. I was feeling suffocated."

Ramon put his hand on her arm to escort her to the door. Deputies posted along the walk, watching everything else. "This must be awful for you. You're welcome to stay in my guest house till this all blows over."

His arm slipped around her, hand on her waist. A bit too low thought Mitch as he walked toward them in the darkness.

"That won't be necessary," said Kate. "Dinner was already too much."

They paused at the door. Ramon could tell it wasn't going anywhere. She was too snooty, too wrapped up in herself to be interested in what he could give her. He knew she wasn't going to accept his offer of a place to stay before he said it, he didn't even have a guest house. He looked out, wondering if he should try to force himself in and saw Mitch. He smiled.

Ramon pulled Kate closer, kissed her and held on so she couldn't break free. She tried, with her hands all over him, and it looked an awful lot like a passionate return kiss to Mitch.

Mitch burst upon them, shoving through the detail and punching Ramon in the side of the head. The little man fell, got his suit dirty, even saw stars.

"What are you doing?" said Kate, glaring at Mitch.

Ramon started laughing. The detail closed in on Mitch, he flushed, cast a quick glance at Kate, walked off.

"Where you going, Kannenberg?" asked Ramon, still laughing, rubbing the side of his head and working up to his feet.

Marci took Mitch's arm, led him to his bike. "You can't be here."

"I know."

"I'll make sure he doesn't stay." She looked at Mitch, there was understanding. "But you're going to make things worse if you don't stay away from her."

Kate fled into the house. Ramon went to his car with an Oscar worthy limp.

Marci said, "Go home. There isn't anybody here who won't say he had it coming."

"Don't do that," said Mitch. "I don't have a good reason to be here." Mitch swung onto the bike. "Why are you here?"

Marci shook her head. "Rask killed five FBI agents this afternoon. They think he might come after the judge." Mitch climbed back off the bike. She shook her head. "Go home. We've got this."

107

Carmen set her bag of take-out from Thai Again on the kitchen table. She liked their noodles and her girlfriend at the health department said they were about the best choice if you had to buy Thai from anywhere.

She kicked off her shoes and looked around. Her apartment was dull. It was late and she had no plans. She had nothing going on the next day either, just work. Always work.

She watched an episode of "Burning Love" and felt very alone. Each episode ended with everybody with somebody. They'd look at each other, the music would play, and then sex. Which is to say she presumed they all had sex because in the next episode they'd gossip about it. She didn't have anyone to look at like that. Hadn't in quite a while.

She thought of Lonnie.

That threw her off. She got up and popped a can of hard cider. Kept thinking about Lonnie. The more she thought about it, the more exciting he became. A street tough turned respectable business man?

She went to sleep thinking about him. In her dreams he looked at her that way. And she looked back. And all the girls at the office gossiped about them the next day. And in that dream she was happy.

108

Mitch was too worked up about Pete, about the suspension, and if he were honest, about Kate, for his next stop to be home. It was Gillian's and he spent a long time there. Empty shot glasses formed ranks around a towering pint glass on the bar in front of him. Other than Gillian herself, the rest of the place was mostly deserted.

Venus came in, walked straight to Mitch and took the stool beside him. He looked rough. "I think I liked it better when you didn't care," she said.

He grunted, gave Gillian an accusing stare. "You call her?" Gillian went further down the bar.

Venus said, "Come on, I'll take you home." She pulled him off the stool. He stumbled a little, was feeling the drink but wasn't numb yet. The TV caught his eye and he held his ground. Venus looked up.

A reporter posed for the camera, a burning house, identified on the bottom of the screen as belonging to Assistant United States Attorney Terrance Gaff, behind her. They were linking it to the attack on an FBI safe house in a quiet residential neighborhood earlier in the day.

Venus called to Gillian. "Two coffees, please." Then she got on her phone.

The coffee helped and by the time Chris and Chuck showed up, Mitch felt more like himself. He was surprised when the Chief walked in.

"Steve's at the judge's house," he said, sitting down across from Venus and Mitch.

"What are we doing?" asked Mitch.

"Somebody needs to stop Rask," said Chuck.

"Chief?" said Venus.

"FBI won't release the warrant but the PD is specifically looking for Jet so the way I see it, you would be helping them." He took a coffee. "Not poaching."

"But that's not how Kurt will see it," said Mitch. Chief agreed.

Venus had a call and took it. They waited until she finished. "Rask is looking for muscle," she said. "He's cruising, keeps popping in places. Everybody's talking about it."

"He's going after Kate," said Mitch. They looked at him. "Judge Silver."

"There's a detail on her," said Chief.

"Double it," said Mitch. "And we should move her."

Chief shook his head. "No 'we' here Kannenberg, you're suspended."

Chuck said, "What if you postpone that for a couple of days?"

Chief said, "No can do. Not to support the detail."

"It wouldn't be to support the detail," said Venus. "Put him on the protective investigation. Your whole district is working this right now and you need everybody, especially your best investigator."

Chief considered that, said, "Okay, here's the play. Mitch is reinstated to work up a location for Rask with you." He looked at the deputies. "All of you are responsible for making sure he behaves. No arrest. No hands on. And absolutely under no circumstance are you to go to the detail site."

Mitch said, "Understood, Sir. Thank you."

Chief got up. "You are behind the scenes."

109

Venus drove the black Explorer with Mitch literally riding shotgun. Chris and Chuck sat in the back, laptops open. Searching.

Everywhere they went folks had talked to Jet, been offered money to join his new crew. Big money but nothing up front. The people they interviewed had turned the offer down, too many people dying, too many empty promises from Jet in the past. The marshals grew hopeful that nobody would sign on, they'd have another day to find him. But they all knew better.

Venus was frustrated. "Do your Voodoo already, Boys. Where is he?"

Chris was edgy, nervous and feeling impotent in front of her. "Keep your panties on. He's making calls, which we see, but then he keeps turning his phone off and moving so-"

Chuck cut him off. "He's making another call." Chuck studied the display, a map of the city with his location marked and then a pinging icon where the call was being made. On the far right a column of coordinates and other data about the phone updated. "It's another cell."

Chris, hoping for redemption, said, "What's the number? I'll plug it into Domo-Babel. We should be able to decrypt the VOIP packets and hear what he's saying."

"We don't have a warrant for that," said Mitch.

Chris looked over at Chuck's screen, got the data he needed. Chuck said, "This isn't going to be evidence, Boss."

Venus said, "There's a line." Mitch nodded, more in thought than agreement.

Chris had been typing furiously and stopped suddenly. "He's talking to Restrepo."

Silence. Venus stared straight ahead. Chuck said, "Mitch?"

"Are you insane?" asked Venus. "That's attorney client privilege. I'm not going to lose my job over Rask."

She was the only one against. Even Mitch's indecision wasn't really dissent. "He's moving," said Chuck.

"What about Kate?" asked Mitch. His voice cracked. The strain of the last week, of all things lost, a hope for absolution.

Venus pulled violently into an empty gas station and skidded to a stop. Her knuckles were white on the steering wheel. She wouldn't look at Mitch. Chris's mouth was open as he read the text scrolling on his screen. Chuck tracked Jet's movement.

"Tell me this is not about locking up Rask," said Venus.

Mitch kept quiet, looked at her until she faced him. No walls, no bull shit.

"Fine," she said with a dark, quiet power that gave Chris the chills. "But it's not for Kate." She pulled back out onto the roadway, hopping a curb. "It's for you."

Chris looked at Chuck, who nodded, and then said, "Restrepo asks what he wants. Jet wants to know where the judge lives. Restrepo asks why and Jet says he's going to kill two birds with one stone. Restrepo says he doesn't want any more details." Chris paused, "Then he gives her up."

The weight of it settles on him. This is real. Life or death and he's in the middle of it. The big time.

Venus turned on the siren. The night sped by. Mitch stared at it through the tinted window and stroked the Remington 870 in his lap. He saw only Jet.

110

The sky drifted out of blackness over Katherine's house. A deputy marshal walking the yard paused to look up, his M-4 slung comfortably in easy reach. Another deputy sat in a car parked at the curb. Both startled, alert.

A car drove slowly down the street, hesitated, and turned left at the end of the block. The deputy in the car made a note on his log sheet. They both relaxed.

The black Explorer pulled in behind the marshals' car on the street. The team dismounted and advanced on the house, passing a third marshal's car in the driveway, parked facing out.

Marci met them at the door with a shotgun, frowning at Mitch. She let them inside. The rooms were still stacked with boxes, a Nook sat on a chair in the hallway.

Mitch started for the stairs. Venus stopped him. "I'll go."

"But-"

"Do you trust me?" she asked. Marci wanted to object to the whole thing. Mitch gestured Venus to the stairs, his face daring anyone to argue. Venus took the stairs two at a time. Chris watched Venus disappear. Then Chuck led both of them to the kitchen.

111

Jet was irritated he couldn't round up a posse. There was a time when people would have worked for him days on end without even being offered money. Now they wanted to see it up front.

He waited alone in Wiggins's car. He was antsy and didn't like sitting still. He felt vulnerable and wasn't sure he could trust his number two anymore. He reached for the can of nuts but there wasn't one.

Four Escalades, tricked out with chrome and custom paint, pulled in around him. He pulled out his pistols. Then saw Wiggins get out of one of the SUVs and relaxed. He put down the window.

"Let's go," said Wiggins. "We're losing night."

Jet smiled. Slipped the guns back in their holsters and climbed out of the Benz. "These guys any good?" Wiggins laughed. Jet saw the cold faces of the men. "Where'd you find them?"

"You want details or revenge?"

Jet climbed into the lead vehicle. Wiggins drove. Four trucks. Sixteen men ready to kill.

112

A dark blue Taurus, emergency lights flashing, screeched to the curb at Judge Silver's house. Pete jumped out and ran inside balancing a pair of take-out coffee cups as he waved to the perimeter team.

He found Mitch in the kitchen with the rest of the detail, offered him one of the cups. Mitch accepted the peace offering gratefully.

Venus helped Kate into body armor. Around them weapons and magazines were being checked and double checked. Jet was coming. It was time to earn their pay.

Day shift arrived amid crackling radios and subdued greetings. Brought the total up to ten deputies. Steve Hart took tactical control from Marci, gave Mitch a warning look, sort of "We both know you aren't supposed to be here but I need another shooter so don't mess this up" and briefed out the plan.

Pete and Mitch slipped aside. Pete said, "You okay?"

"Yeah."

"I've got this," said Pete. He did.

"I know."

Pete looked over at Kate. "You really think you and her?"

Mitch said, "Thanks for the coffee."

113

The Escalades traded highway for a residential neighborhood just as it was waking up. The men were serious, their weapons out. Jet grinned like a kid heading to a backroad turnoff after prom, or a madman.

A few blocks away, Mitch stood in Kate's driveway and slammed shut the rear door of the Expedition. He sprinted around to the driver's seat and pulled out, everyone else already saddled up.

The Taurus took off. Mitch eased out of the driveway and then the Escalades were there, everything became shooting and squealing tires. One of the follow cars was caught out of formation and disabled by Jet's crew. The deputies inside bailed and returned fire from cover. Windows shattered but the Escalades moved on.

The rest of the motorcade rocketed away, lights flashing, sirens blaring, and guns blazing. The marshals ran fast, Mitch pushed as hard as he could without losing his tail cover. The follow cars ran double, blocking the narrow street between the houses. Every time an Escalade took to a lawn to get by, it fishtailed out of control and had to cut back to the pavement.

They hit the intersection with the highway and Mitch went for it. Traffic was building with the start of morning rush hour and it was hard to keep the formation together. They pushed through red lights, barely slowing, the motorcade twisting through cars, scraping when things got tight, yet somehow managing to avoid game over collisions.

The gunfire was nearly constant, civilian vehicles caught in the middle were run off the road with crunched bodywork and shattered windows as the gangsters bumped and shot their way through. One of the Escalades pulled up on the shoulder, cut back in sharply and sent a motorcycle flying across the roadway.

Jet screamed continuously. Wiggins slid along the sides of cars and pushed drivers out of his way. He slowed when he came up to a school bus. Jet fumed, stomped his foot down on Wiggins's and they careened around, bouncing against the side and leaving a yellow mark on the Escalade.

Jet's gang rammed the follow cars and sent them bouncing out of control, shots going wild. Broken glass and bullet fragments left everyone bloodied. The marshals moved into single file to slip through a line of traffic. The stopped cars surprised Wiggins who swerved hard to avoid them and bounced along the side of the road, smashing between the Jersey barrier and the line of cars. They fell back.

A rifle tracked the remaining Escalades from the rear marshal's car, firing accurately and doing damage to the men pursuing. The trucks split, one taking to the inside shoulder. The driver spotted an opening and jerked his wheel, smashing unexpectedly against the rear of the follow car. The vehicles locked together, spun while the other Escalades zoomed by. The two cars twirled, exchanging fire in a billowing cloud of black smoke. When the cars stopped, the fight was over.

Chris and Marci leaped from the mangled car, their back seater a beat behind. Chris commandeered the first functioning car in the row of carnage beside them, a powder blue Prius. Marci grabbed her shot gun and followed him while the back seater cuffed the bodies in the mangled Escalade together and waited for it all to be over.

They sped off, Marci shaking her head. "A Prius?"

Chris said, "What's wrong with a Prius? Chicks love these things."

One by one the cars dropped off until it was just Mitch with Jet on his tail. Traffic was too thick, he couldn't keep his speed so he dove off the highway onto an access road. Wiggins kept Jet right behind.

Jet told him to go faster. Both cars were damaged, had men bleeding out inside. They cut through side streets and alleys, then through parking lots and into oncoming traffic. Mitch was good, but not good enough. Wiggins held on.

They cut into a lumber yard and Wiggins pulled out to the side. Jet fired repeatedly and Mitch lost a tire. He fishtailed into a T-stop against an embankment. The Escalade sped by and turned to come back with a spray of gravel.

Mitch and Chuck ran from the car dragging their protectee up the embankment. The Escalade plowed into the marshal's car, doors opened, and Jet and Wiggins hit the ground shooting at the retreating marshals. The gangsters followed them on foot, Wiggins keeping low and Jet strutting forward.

Cover was sparse. Mitch and Chuck were low on ammunition, trying to stay down, to keep her covered. Jet and Wiggins moved in close. The marshals fired down, emptied their magazines, Mitch looked for a way out.

No place to go. "This is my last one," said Chuck, popping in a magazine.

"Mine too," said Mitch. They could hear Jet coming. Calling out to them. And laughing.

Chuck threw a rock. It hit Jet. "A rock? Are you kidding?"

Wiggins stuck his head out to look. Chuck was already aimed in, double tapped him in the head. Jet drew a bead on Chuck and fired before Wiggins hit the ground. Chuck staggered and was hit again by the powerful .45. He stumbled back and fell. Jet's slide locked back, empty.

Jet pulled out a knife, looked around. "Let's get this over with, Kannenberg,"

"I'm right here," said Mitch. Jet ran toward the sound. Mitch took a deep breath then stood, fired all 13 rounds in two and a quarter seconds. Half of them struck the man but none stopped him.

They came together, fast and brutal. Jet was strong and ferocious. Mitch was hungover. The knife cut him over and over as they fought, each time a little deeper. Mitch was losing.

Jet shoved him down, kicked at him. Then he caught motion out of the corner of his eye and spun, saw the woman sneaking up behind him. He threw her hard against the ground, her head smacked against a rock.

"This is taking too long," said Jet.

"You got a date?" asked Mitch. His face was a mess.

Jet looked back at the woman. "You could say that. I've still got to finish off the judge when I'm done with you."

Mitch struggled to his feet and rushed in, arms flailing, giving it everything he had left. It wasn't enough. Jet beat him back, cut him deep. He couldn't see. Couldn't breathe.

He fell back, Jet towered over him, raised the knife to plunge down through his heart. A shot erupted over the ringing and pounding in Mitch's ears, surprised them both, and Jet dropped, sprawled across him.

Mitch lifted his head and looked across Jet at the woman who knelt on the ground beside Chuck, his pistol held in a perfect grip and still covering Jet. Venus. She locked eyes with Mitch. Scrambled across the rocky ground to Jet and cuffed him, pulled him off. Saw he was dead.

She put her arms around Mitch, tight, and held on. He flopped an arm around her too, but it was weak, he didn't have much left. "We need to get you out of here," she said. He smiled faintly.

A groan. They turned to see Chuck, on his side, working at getting to his knees. His shirt bulged where the ballistic plate of his body armor had been bent out of shape.

The three of them worked their way down the embankment, Mitch slung in the middle. The yard filled with police cars and then an ambulance.

Pete pulled up in the Taurus, stared at the blood matted on Venus's hair, Mitch cut to pieces. He didn't have anything to say, settled for a group hug.

Kate got out of the Taurus too and rushed over to Mitch. She kissed him and he tried to kiss her back and for a moment nothing else mattered.

"It's so beautiful," said Pete.

Venus said, "You'd better change your shirt. Patti's going to kill you if she sees blood on you."

The Prius arrived. Pete asked, "What's that?"

Chris and Marci got out. Venus said, "Nice ride."

Chris smiled at Marci. "Told you."

Steve Hart strode over to where Katherine stood beside Mitch, holding his hand. He was on a stretcher, IV and blood pack emptying into him.

"I hate to break this up, but the Judge is needed in court," said Steve. "There's the small matter of the United States of America versus David Rask to attend to."

114

David Rask didn't look good in orange. The rough canvas jumpsuit hung on him like second hand drapes and itched, made him scratch like he had psoriasis. It also clashed with the blue canvas shoes on his feet. He hadn't slept and already the distinctive odor shared by all of the incarcerated wafted from him. He shifted uncomfortably on the cold stainless steel bench, stared at his attorneys through the wire mesh of the marshal's cell block interview room, and stewed.

The attorneys, well dressed men in their middle forties, were Keegan on the right and Stillman on the left. They paid little attention to the appearance of their client or even his rising anger. He hadn't taken the news of Ramon Restrepo's arrest well, accused the man of being a snake and probably a worse rat than Raj could have been.

Stillman said, "This is bad, Mr. Rask." Keegan nodded. "You may be facing additional charges. The AUSA told us he has a recorded phone conversation between you and Restrepo from the jail yesterday."

David dismissed it. "I didn't say anything. That's bluff."

Keegan said, "You don't have to. It only needs to be suggestive. Your son tried to kill a federal judge, your judge, and he murdered a witness in your case. That call makes it look like you were involved and jurors don't like that."

David was furious. "I'm going to kill that bastard of mine."

Keegan and Stillman exchanged glances. "That won't be necessary," said Stillman, "I'm sorry, but James was killed during his attack on the judge."

The fight drained out of David, his face paled, the flush of anger exchanged for shock. "Dead?"

"We can probably work a deal," said Keegan. "Push most of the enterprise and conspiracy to him. The fraud is going to stick, we can't help that, but the rest, maybe, if we go after it now, maybe we can get you into the 8-10 range."

David felt the grief coming, fought to hold it back for a minute, and gave up. Tears filled his eyes. "10 years?"

Stillman nodded. "That's pretty good, considering your exposure. James has given you an out."

David spoke slowly, the shadow of angry contempt behind his distress. "My son is dead and you tell me I should be happy about getting a deal for 10 years because I can blame him?"

"Mr. Rask," said Keegan, "You do realize that you would most likely have spent the rest of your life in prison? The FBI did a very good job. The case agent was meticulous."

"My son is dead," said Rask, incredulous. "Doesn't that mean anything to you?"

"You didn't hire us to care about your son," said Stillman. "You hired us to get you out of trouble. If you'd like we can ask for a continuance, give you a couple of days to grieve, but you'll lose the advantage and in my opinion, any delay and you'd be lucky to get 15."

David stood, turned away from his counsel. He leaned against the cool brick wall. Resisted the urge to bang his head against it over and over until everything went black. He sat back down. "What do you need from me?"

115

Pete sat in the hospital room beside Mitch. He'd been stitched back up and other than a couple of scrapes on his face and arms, and the ubiquitous IV needle, he looked okay.

"Thanks," said Mitch.

Pete could have said a lot of things that sounded like he was only doing his job, but instead he said, "That's what friends are for."

"Good luck out there. I'll keep your slot open on the squad, for when you get bored."

Pete laughed. "Tell you what, you miss me that much and I'll make a spot on ours for you."

Mitch turned on the TV. News Channel 14 had a special report from the Federal Courthouse. They watched Assistant United States Attorney Terry Gaff and FBI Special Agent Kurt Cunningham walk down the steps for the press conference of their careers. Rask's legal team from New York waited at the doors for their own turn.

"Good day for justice," said Pete. Mitch nodded.

116

Lonnie Perez walked out of the courthouse behind the men speaking to the cameras. He was on thousands of TV screens but hardly anyone noticed him. That was fine with Lonnie, his plans were for fortune, not fame.

Carmen spotted him at the corner and walked over. "Sorry you had to spend the night in jail." He saw she meant it and smiled at her as she went on, "With everything going on I couldn't get it sorted out for you."

"It ain't no thing," said Lonnie. She said, "But a chicken wing?" They both laughed. She looked fine in a light blue sun dress with her hair pulled back and Wayfarer sunglasses.

"Where you headed?" she asked.

"Back to the club. My car's there."

"Want a ride?" Her voice was a little different, a little something extra. He looked closely, caught a spark, a glimpse of something he really liked. She said, "I'm over here."

She led him to her old Rav 4. It was one of the two tone aquamarine ones that had faded almost turquoise. They pulled away from the courthouse. He said, "I didn't think you could give us cons a ride."

She nodded. "Thought you were an ex-con." Flashed him her own smile, full of perfect teeth. "Besides, I don't think anybody's going to notice today." It was how she said that too. Lonnie spent a minute thinking about her a little differently than before. It was just a minute, but he liked thinking about her that way, thought maybe he'd do it some more.

She pulled into Booty Island. There were cops there. A lot of cops. "What are they doing?" she asked. "I thought they had everybody."

Lonnie said, "They're probably looking for Jet's treasure chest."

She thought about that. "Hidden treasure buried at Booty Island?"

Lonnie nodded. Opened the door. "Thanks for the ride."

She smiled at him. Looked back at the cops. "Think they'll find any?"

Lonnie answered carefully, a hint rather than an admission, "No." Her expression changed.

"Because there isn't any buried treasure?" Asked back just as carefully.

He shook his head. "Because it isn't there anymore." He got out. Walked around her car to Big Maggie's Caprice. Carmen's window was down. He started thinking that way again. "You got anything going on?"

"I'm a probation officer."

"That your dream?"

She got out of her car. The dress rode up a little, he caught a quick glimpse of thigh when she swung out. She appraised the Caprice.

"What you said before, about being done, are you?"

He looked at the club. "I'm going to open my own place, nicer than this. On a beach." He opened the passenger door. "I think you'd like it."

She took a deep breath, got in. "Me too." He shut the door, smiling. Climbed in to the driver's side, said, "We just have to make a quick stop."

She looked at him, second thoughts racing as fast as her heart. He said, "Don't want to be guilty of stealing a car."

117

Big Maggie knew about men and women so when her car pulled up with that pretty little thing of a probation officer sitting beside her Lonnie she sighed a deep sigh.

They waved from the street, walked up the walk and even though they weren't hanging on each other, it was pretty clear they were an item.

"I see your boss had a bad night," said Maggie.

"We're heading out," said Lonnie. "I wanted to swing by, see what you needed."

"Aren't you sweet," said Maggie.

"I'm serious," said Lonnie. He sat beside her on the porch glider.

"I know you are, Baby." She patted his hand. "You cleaned up real good."

"So what do you need before I go?"

She batted her eyes and smiled for Carmen. "I don't need nothing, thank you. You know how the Lord always provides."

Lonnie nodded. "You interested in selling me your old car?"

"It's not an old car."

"I'm afraid it is," said Lonnie. "Old junker, really."

"Classic," said Maggie. "Runs like a dream. Holds all my groceries. You buy yourself a new car and leave mine out of your enterprise."

Lonnie stretched, said, "I don't want a new car and if I'm going to buy an old car I want it to be yours."

"Not for sale," said Maggie.

"Everything's for sale," said Lonnie. "What's your price?"

The negotiations were long and fierce and Carmen loved every minute. Maggie finally settled for $300k, robbery, she said, for such a nice old car. And cash too, she said, because she didn't trust no check from a man like Lonnie even if he did say he was cleaned up. And for the love of God he'd better treat that nice girl right.

Lonnie smiled at her through it all. "I'm going to miss you, Maggie."

She erupted in tears. "Get out of here you old hoodlum." Carmen hugged her and the old woman said, "He's one of the good ones. You'll be okay."

They got into the car. Carmen said, "Just how big is that treasure chest?"

Lonnie grinned. "See? That's the kind of worry you'll never have again."

118

It was late. Venus sat quietly beside Mitch's hospital bed, chair pulled up against it, holding his hand and staring at him. He slept. Both of their faces bruised.

Nobody walking by could misunderstand what passed between them, what years of being together most of everyday let them say without speaking. Or even being awake.

Kate paused on her way through the doorway when she saw them. Watched Venus raise his hand to her lips.

Kate slipped away, wiped a little moisture from the bridge of her nose. It never could have worked anyway. They both knew that. Right?

End